Something had thrown Earth's scientists into an uproar—or rather, *nothing* had. Because suddenly there was absolutely *nothing* where something very definitely should have been.

Phobos and Deimos, the two moons of mars, had disappeared.

And that was just the start of it. Before long, more of the solar system's moons were gone . . . people on Earth were sinking out of sight into the ground . . . and Earth's telepaths kept having strange dreams, full of foreboding . . .

DR. KOMETEVSKY'S DAY is just one of the exciting, imaginative stories in this great collection of stories by award-winning master of science-fiction, Fritz Leiber.

SHIPS
TO THE
STARS

FRITZ LEIBER

ace books
A Division of Charter Communications Inc.
A GROSSET & DUNLAP COMPANY
1120 Avenue of the Americas
New York, New York 10036

An ACE Book

Table of Contents

DR. KOMETEVSKY'S DAY

"But it's all predicted here! It even names this century for the next reshuffling of the planets."

Celeste Wolver looked up unwillingly at the book her friend Madge Carnap held aloft like a torch. She made out the ill-stamped title, *The Dance of the Planets*. There was no mistaking the time of it's origin; only paper from the Twentieth Century aged to that particularly nasty shade of brown. Indeed, the book seemed to Celeste a brown old witch resurrected from the Last Age of Madness to confound a world growing sane, and she couldn't help shrinking back a trifle toward her husband Theodor.

He tried to come to her rescue. "Only predicted in the vaguest way. As I understand it, Kometevsky claimed, on the basis of a lot of evidence drawn from folklore, that the planets and their moons trade positions every so often."

"As if they were playing Going to Jerusalem, or musical chairs," Celeste chimed in, but she couldn't make it sound funny.

"Jupiter was supposed to have started as the outermost planet, and is to end up in the orbit of Mercury," Theodor continued. "Well, nothing at all like that has happened."

"But it's begun," Madge said with conviction. "Phobos and Deimos have disappeared. You can't argue away that stubborn little fact."

That was the trouble; you couldn't..Mars' two tiny moons had simply vanished during a period when,

1

as was generally the case, the eyes of astronomy weren't on them. Just some hundred-odd cubic miles of rock—the merest cosmic flyspecks—yet they had carried away with them the security of a whole world.

Looking at the lovely garden landscape around her, Celeste Wolver felt that in a moment the shrubby hills would begin to roll like waves, the charmingly aimless paths twist like snakes and sink in the green sea, the sparsely placed skyscrapers dissolve into the misty clouds they pierced.

People must have felt like this, she thought, *when Aristarches first hinted and Copernicus told them that the solid Earth under their feet was falling dizzily through space. Only it's worse for us, because they couldn't see that anything had changed. We can.*

"You need something to cling to," she heard Madge say. "Dr. Kometevsky was the only person who ever had an inkling that anything like this might happen. I was never a Kometevskyite before. Hadn't even heard of the man."

She said it almost apologetically. In fact, standing there so frank and anxious-eyed, Madge looked anything but a fanatic, which made it much worse.

"Of course, there are several more convincing alternate explanations . . ." Theodor began hesitantly, knowing very well that there weren't. If Phobos and Deimos had suddenly disintegrated, surely Mars Base would have noticed something. Of course there was the Disordered Space Hypothesis, even if it was little more than the chance phrase of a prominent physicist pounded upon by an eager journalist. And in any case, what sense of security were you

2

left with if you admitted that moons and planets might explode, or drop through unseen holes in space? So he ended up by taking a different tack: "Besides, if Phobos and Deimos simply shot off somewhere, surely they'd have been picked up by now by 'scope or radar."

"Two balls of rock just a few miles in diameter?" Madge questioned. "Aren't they smaller than many of the asteroids? I'm no astronomer, but I think I'm right."

And of course she was.

She swung the book under her arm. "Whew, it's heavy," she observed, adding in slightly scandalized tones, "Never been microfilmed." She smiled nervously and looked them up and down. "Going to a party?" she asked.

Theodor's scarlet cloak and Celeste's green culottes and silver jacket justified the question, but they shook their heads.

"Just the normally flamboyant garb of the family." Celeste said, while Theodor explained, "As it happens, we're bound on business connected with the disappearance. We Wolvers practically constitute a sub-committee of the Congress for the Discovery of New Purposes. And since a lot of varied material comes to our attention, we're going to see if any of it correlates with this bit of astronomical sleight-of-hand."

Madge nodded. "Give you something to do, at any rate. Well, I must be off. The Buddhist temple has lent us their place for a meeting." She gave them a woeful grin. "See you when the Earth jumps."

Theodor said to Celeste, "Come on, dear. We'll be late."

3

But Celeste didn't want to move too fast. "You know, Teddy," she said uncomfortably, "all this reminds me of those old myths where too much good fortune is a sure sign of coming disaster. It was just too much good luck, our great-grandparents missing World III and getting the World Government started a thousand years ahead of schedule. Luck like that couldn't last, evidently. Maybe we've gone too fast with a lot of things, like space-flight and the Deep Shaft and—" she hesitated a bit—"complex marriages. I'm a woman. I want complete security. Where am I to find it?"

"In me," Theodor said promptly.

"In you?" Celeste questioned, walking slowly. "But you're just one-third of my husband. Perhaps I should look for it in Edmund or Ivan."

"You angry with me about something?"

"Of course not. But a woman wants her source of security whole. In a crisis like this, it's disturbing to have it divided."

"Well, we are a whole and, I believe, indivisible family," Theodor told her warmly. "You're not suggesting, are you, that we're going to be punished for our polygamous sins by a cosmic catastrophe? Fire from heaven and all that?"

"Don't be silly. I just wanted to give you a picture of my feeling." Celeste smiled. "I guess none of us realized how much we've come to depend on the idea of unchanging scientific law. Knocks the props from under you."

Theodor nodded emphatically. "All the more reason to get a line on what's happening as quickly as possible. You know, it's fantastically far-fetched but I think the experience of persons with Extra-Sensory

4

Perception may give us a clue. During the past three or four days there's been a remarkable similarity in the dreams of ESPs all over the planet. I'm going to present the evidence at the meeting."

Celeste looked up at him. "So that's why Rosalind's bringing Frieda's daughter?"

"Dotty is your daughter, too, and Rosalind's," Theodor reminded her.

"No, just Frieda's," Celeste said bitterly. Of course you may be the father. One-third of a chance."

Theodor looked at her sharply, but didn't comment. "Anyway, Dotty will be there," he said. "Probably asleep by now. All the ESPs have suddenly seemed to need more sleep."

As they talked, it had been growing darker, though the luminescence of the path kept it from being bothersome. And now the cloud rack parted to the east, showing a single red planet low on the horizon.

"Did you know," Theodor said suddenly, "that in *Gulliver's Travels* Dean Swift predicted that better telescopes would show Mars to have two moons? He got the sizes and distances and periods damned accurately, too. One of the few really startling coincidences of reality and literature."

"Stop being eerie," Celeste said sharply. But then she went on, "Those names Phobos and Deimos— they're Greek, aren't they? What do they mean?"

Theodor lost a step. "Fear and Terror," he said unwillingly. "Now don't go taking that for an omen. Most of the mythological names of major and minor ancient gods had been taken—the bodies in the Solar System are named that way, of course—and these were about all that were available."

It was true, but it didn't comfort him much.

I am a God, Dotty was dreaming, *and I want to be by myself and think. I and my god-friends like to keep some of our thoughts secret, but the other gods have forbidden us to.*

A little smile flickered across the lips of the sleeping girl, and the woman in gold tights and gold-spangled jacket leaned forward thoughtfully. In her dignity and simplicity and straight-spined grace, she was rather like a circus mother watching her sick child before she went out for the trapeze act.

I and my god-friends sail off in our great round silver boats, Dotty went on dreaming. *The other gods are angry and scared. They are frightened of the thoughts we may think in secret. They follow us to hunt us down. There are many more of them than of us.*

As Celeste and Theodor entered the committee room, Rosalind Wolver—a glitter of platinum against darkness—came in through the opposite door and softly shut it behind her. Frieda, a fair woman in blue robes, got up from the round table.

Celeste turned away with outward casualness as Theodor kissed his two other wives. She was pleased to note that Edmund seemed impatient too. A figure in close-fitting black, unrelieved except for two red arrows at the collar, he struck her as embodying very properly the serious, fateful temper of the moment.

He took two briefcases from his vest pocket and tossed them down on the table beside one of the microfilm projectors.

"I suggest we get started without waiting for Ivan," he said. Frieda frowned anxiously. "It's ten minutes since he phoned from the Deep Space Bar to say he was starting right away. And that's hardly two minutes walk."

Rosalind instantly started toward the outside door.

"I'll check," she explained. "Oh, Frieda, I've set the mike so you'll hear if Dotty calls."

Edmund threw up his hands. "Very well, then," he said and walked over, switched on the picture and stared out moodily.

Theodor and Frieda got out their briefcases, switched on projectors, and began silently checking through their material.

Celeste fiddled with the TV and got a newscast. But she found her eyes didn't want to absorb the blocks of print that rather swiftly succeeded each other, so, after a few moments, she shrugged impatiently and switched to audio.

At the noise, the others looked around at her with surprise and some irritation, but in a few moments they were also listening.

"The two rocket ships sent out from Mars Base to explore the orbital positions of Phobos and Deimos— that is, the volume of space they'd be occupying if their positions had remained normal—report finding masses of dust and larger debris. The two masses of fine debris are moving in the same orbits and at the same velocities as the two vanished moons, and occupy roughly the same volumes of space, though the mass of material is hardly a hundredth that of the moons. Physicists have ventured no statements as to whether this constitutes a confirmation of the Disintegration Hypothesis.

"However, we're mighty pleased at this news here. There's a marked lessening of tension. The finding of

7

the debris—solid, tangible stuff—seems to lift the whole affair out of the supernatural miasma in which some of us have been tempted to plunge it. One-hundredth of the moons has been found.

"The rest will also be!"

Edmund had turned his back on the window. Frieda and Theodor had switched off their projectors.

"Meanwhile, Earthlings are going about their business with a minimum of commotion, meeting with considerable calm the strange threat to the fabric of their Solar System. Many, of course, are assembled in churches and humanist temples. Kometevskyites have staged helicopter processions at Washington, Peking, Pretoria, and Christiana, demanding that instant preparations be made for—and I quote—'Earth's coming leap through space.' They have also formally challenged all astronomers to produce an explanation other than the one contained in that strange book so recently conjured from oblivion, *The Dance of the Planets.*

"That about winds up the story for the present. There are no new reports from Interplanetary Radar Astronomy, or the other rocket ships searching in the extended Mars volume. Nor have any statements been issued by the various groups working on the problem in Astrophysics, Cosmic Ecology, the Congress for the Discovery of New Purposes, and so forth. Meanwhile, however, we can take courage from the words of a poem written even before Dr. Kometevsky's book:

"This Earth is not the steadfast place
We landsmen build upon;
From deep to deep she varies pace,

8

And while she comes is gone.
Beneath my feet I feel
Her smooth bulk heave and dip;
With velvet plunge and soft upreel
She swings and steadies to her keel
Like a gallant, gallant ship.' "

While the TV voice intoned the poem, growing
richer as emotion caught it up, Celeste looked around
her at the others. Frieda, with her touch of feminine
helplessness showing more than ever through her
businesslike poise. Theodor leaning forward from his
scarlet cloak thrown back, smiling the half-smile with
which he seemed to face even the unknown. Black
Edmund, masking a deep uncertainty with a strong
show of decisiveness.

In short, her family. She knew their every quirk
and foible. And yet now they seemed to her a million
miles away, figures seen through the wrong end of
a telescope.

Where they really a family? Strong sources of mu-
tual strength and security to each other? Or had they
merely been playing family, experimenting with
their notions of complex marriage like a bunch of
silly adolescents? Butterflies taking advantage of
good weather to wing together in a glamorous, arti-
ficial dance—until outraged Nature decided to wipe
them out?

As the poem was ending, Celeste saw the door
open and Rosalind come slowly in. The Golden Woman's face was white as the paths she had been
treading.

Just then the TV voice quickened with shock.
"News! Lunar Observatory One reports that, al-

9

though Jupiter is just about to pass behind the Sun, a good coronagraph of the planet has been obtained. Checked and rechecked, it admits of only one interpretation, which Lunar One feels duty-bound to release. *Jupiter's fourteen moons are no longer visible!"*

The chorus of remarks with which the Wolvers would otherwise have received this was checked by one thing: the fact that Rosalind seemed not to hear it. Whatever was on her mind prevented even that incredible statement from penetrating.

She walked shakily to the table and put down a briefcase, one end of which was smudged with dirt.

Without looking at them, she said, "Ivan left the Deep Space Bar twenty minutes ago, said he was coming straight here. On my way back I searched the path. Midway I found this half-buried in the dirt. I had to tug to get it out—almost as if it had been cemented into the ground. Do you feel how the dirt seems to be *in* the leather, as if it had lain for years in the grave?"

By now the others were fingering the small case of microfilms they had seen so many times in Ivan's competent hands. What Rosalind said was true. It had a gritty, unwholesome feel to it. Also, it felt strangely heavy.

"And see what's written on it," she added.

They turned it over. Scrawled with white pencil in big, hasty, frantic letters were two words:

"Going down!"

The other gods, Dotty dreamt, *are combing the whole Universe for us. We have escaped them many times, but now our tricks are almost used up. There are no doors going out of the Universe and our boats are silver beacons to the hunters. So we decide to disguise them in the only way they can be disguised. It is our last chance.*

Edmund rapped the table to gain the family's attention.

"I'd say we've done everything we can for the moment to find Ivan. We've made a thorough local search. A wider one, which we can't conduct personally, is in progress. All helpful agencies have been alerted and descriptions are being broadcast. I suggest we get on with the business of the evening—which may very well be connected with Ivan's disappearance."

One by one the others nodded and took their places at the round table. Celeste made a great effort to throw off the feeling of unreality that had engulfed her and focus attention on her microfilms.

"I'll take over Ivan's notes," she heard Edmund say. "They're mainly about the Deep Shaft."

"How far have they got with that?" Frieda asked idly. "Twenty-five miles?"

"Near thirty, I believe," Edmund answered, "and still going down."

At those last two words they all looked up quickly. Then their eyes went toward Ivan's briefcase.

Our trick has succeeded, Dotty dreamt. *The other gods have passed our hiding place a dozen times without noticing. They search the Universe for us many times in vain. They finally decide that we have found a door going out of the Universe. Yet they fear us all the more. They think of us as devils who will*

11

*some day return through the door to destroy them.
So they watch everywhere. We lie quietly smiling
in our camouflaged boats, yet hardly daring to move
or think, for fear that the faintest echoes of our do-
ings will give them a clue. Hundreds of millions of
years pass by. They seem to us no more than drugged
hours in a prison.*

Theodor rubbed his eyes and pushed his chair
back from the table. "We need a break."

Frieda agreed wearily. "We've gone through everything."

"Good idea," Edmund said briskly. "I think we've
hit on several crucial points along the way and half
disentangled them from the great mass of incon-
sequential material. I'll finish up that part of the job
right now and present my case when we're all a bit
fresher. Say half an hour?"

Theodor nodded heavily, pushing up from his
chair and hitching his cloak over a shoulder.

"I'm going out for a drink," he informed them.

After several hesitant seconds, Rosalind quietly
followed him. Frieda stretched out on a couch and
closed her eyes. Edmund scanned microfilms tire-
lessly, every now and then setting one aside.

Celeste watched him for a minute, then sprang
up and started toward the room where Dotty was
asleep. But midway she stopped.

Not my child, she thought bitterly. *Frieda's her
mother, Rosalind her nurse. I'm nothing at all. Just
one of the husband's girl friends. A lady of uneasy
virtue in a dissolving world.*

But then she straightened her shoulders and went
on.

Rosalind didn't catch up with Theodor. Her footsteps were silent and he never looked back along the path whose feeble white glow rose only knee-high, lighting a low strip of shrub and mossy tree-trunk to either side, no more.

It was a little chilly. She drew on her gloves, but she didn't hurry. In fact, she fell farther and farther behind the dipping tail of his scarlet cloak and his plodding red shoes, which seemed to move disembodied, like those in the fairy tale.

When she reached the point where she had found Ivan's briefcase, she stopped altogether.

A breeze rustled the leaves, and, moistly brushing her cheek, brought forest scents of rot and mold. After a bit she began to hear the furtive scurryings and scuttlings of forest creatures.

She looked around her half-heartedly, suddenly realizing the futility of her quest. What clues could she hope to find in this knee-high twilight? And they'd thoroughly combed the place earlier in the night.

Without warning, an eerie tingling went through her and she was seized by a horror of the cold, grainy Earth underfoot—an ancestral terror from the days when men shivered at ghost stories about graves and tombs.

A tiny detail persisted in bulking larger and larger in her mind—the unnaturalness of the way the Earth had impregnated the corner of Ivan's briefcase, almost as if dirt and leather co-existed in the same space. She remembered the queer way the partly buried briefcase had resisted her first tug, like a rooted plant.

She felt cowed by the mysterious night about her,

13

and literally dwarfed, as if she had grown several inches shorter. She roused herself and started forward.

Something held her feet.

They were ankle-deep in the path. While she looked in fright and horror, they began to sink still lower into the ground.

She plunged frantically, trying to jerk loose. She couldn't. She had the panicky feeling that the Earth had not only trapped but invaded her; that its molecules were creeping up between the molecules of her flesh; that the two were becoming one.

And she was sinking faster. Now knee-deep, thigh-deep, hip-deep, waist-deep. She beat at the powdery path with her hands and threw her body from side to side in agonized frenzy like some sinner frozen in the ice of the innermost circle of the ancients' hell. And always the sense of the dark, grainy tide rose inside as well as around her.

She thought, *he'd just have had time to scribble that note on his briefcase and toss it away.* She jerked off a glove, leaned out as far as she could, and made a frantic effort to drive its fingers into the powdery path. Then the Earth mounted to her chin, her nose, and covered her eyes.

She expected blackness, but it was as if the light of the path stayed with her, making a little glow all around. She saw roots, pebbles, black rot, worn tunnels, worms. Tier on tier of them, her vision penetrating the solid ground. And at the same time, the knowledge that these same sorts of things were coursing up through her.

And still she continued to sink at a speed that increased, as if the law of gravitation applied to her in a diminished way. She dropped from soil through gray clay and into pale limestone.

Her tortured, rock-permeated lungs sucked at rock and drew in air. She wondered madly if a volume of air were falling with her through the stone.

A glitter of quartz. The momentary openness of a foot-high cavern with a trickle of water. And then she was sliding down a black basalt column, half inside it, half inside goldflecked ore. Then just black basalt. And always faster.

It grew hot, then hotter, as if she were approaching the mythical eternal fires.

At first glance Theodor thought the Deep Space Bar was empty. Then he saw a figure hunched monkeylike on the last stool, almost lost in the blue shadows, while behind the bar, her crystal dress blending with the tiers of sparkling glasses, stood a grave-eyed young girl who could hardly have been fifteen.

The TV was saying, ". . . in addition, a number of mysterious disappearances of high-rating individuals have been reported. These are thought to be cases of misunderstanding, illusory apprehension, and impulse traveling—a result of the unusual stresses of the time. Finally, a few suggestible individuals in various parts of the globe, especially the Indian Peninsula, have declared themselves to be 'gods' and in some way responsible for current events.

"It is thought—"

The girl switched off the TV and took Theodor's order, explaining casually, "Joe wanted to go to a Kometevskyite meeting, so I took over for him."

When she had prepared Theodor's highball, she announced, "I'll have a drink with you gentlemen," and squeezed herself a glass of pomegranate juice.

The monkeylike figure muttered, "Scotch-and-soda," then turned toward Edmund and asked, "And what is your reaction to all this, sir?"

Theodor recognized the shrunken wrinkle-seamed face. It was Colonel Fortescue; a military antique long retired from the Peace Patrol and reputed to have seen actual fighting in the Last Age of Madness. Now, for some reason, the face sported a knowing smile.

Theodor shrugged. Just then the TV "big news" light blinked blue and the girl switched on audio. The Colonel winked at Theodor.

". . . confirming the disappearance of Jupiter's moons. But two other utterly fantastic reports have just been received. First, Lunar Observatory One says that it is visually tracking fourteen small bodies which it believes may be the lost moons of Jupiter. They are moving outward from the Solar System at an incredible velocity and are already beyond the orbit of Saturn!"

The Colonel said, "Ah!"

"Second, Palomar reports a large number of dark bodies approaching the Solar System at an equally incredible velocity. They are at about twice the distance of Pluto, but closing in fast! We will be on the air with further details as soon as possible."

The Colonel said, "Ah-ha!"

Theodor stared at him. The old man's self-satisfied poise was almost amusing.

"Are you a Kometevskyite?" Theodor asked him.

The Colonel laughed. "Of course not, my boy. Those poor people are fumbling in the dark. Don't you see what's happened?"

"Frankly, no."

The Colonel leaned toward Theodor and whispered gruffly, "The Divine Plan. God is a military strategist, naturally."

Then he lifted the scotch-and-soda in his clawlike hand and took a satisfying swallow.

"I knew it all along, of course," he went on musingly, "but this last news makes it as plain as a rocket blast, at least to anyone who knows military strategy. Look here, my boy, suppose you were commanding a fleet and got wind of the enemy's approach—what would you do? Why, you'd send your scouts and destroyers fanning out toward them. Behind that screen you'd mass your heavy ships. Then—"

"You don't mean to imply—" Theodor interrupted.

The girl behind the bar looked at them both cryptically.

"Of course I do!" the Colonel cut in sharply. "It's a war between the forces of good and evil. The bright suns and planets are on one side, the dark on the other.

"The moons are the destroyers, Jupiter and Saturn are the big battleships, while we're on a heavy cruiser, I'm proud to say. We'll probably go into action soon. Be a corking fight, what? And all by divine strategy!"

He chuckled and took another big drink. Theodor looked at him sourly. The girl behind the bar polished a glass and said nothing.

Dotty suddenly began to turn and toss, and a look

of terror came over her sleeping face. Celeste leaned forward apprehensively.

The child's lips worked and Celeste made out the sleepy-fuzzy words: "They've found out where we're hiding. They're coming to get us. No! Please, no!"

Celeste's reactions were mixed. She felt worried about Dotty and at the same time almost in terror of her, as if the little girl were an agent of supernatural forces. She told herself that this fear was an expression of her own hostility, yet she didn't really believe it. She touched the child's hand.

Dotty's eyes opened without making Celeste feel she had quite come awake. After a bit she looked at Celeste and her little lips parted in a smile.

"Hello," she said sleepily. "I've been having such funny dreams." Then, after a pause, frowning, "I really am a god, you know. It feels very queer."

"Yes, dear?" Celeste prompted uneasily. "Shall I call Frieda?"

The smile left Dotty's lips. "Why do you act so nervous around me?" she asked. "Don't you love me, Mummy?"

Celeste started at the word. Her throat closed. Then, very slowly, her face broke into a radiant smile. "Of course I do, darling. I love you very much."

Dotty nodded happily, her eyes already closed again.

There was a sudden flurry of excited voices beyond the door. Celeste heard her name called. She stood up.

"I'm going to have to go out and talk with the others," she said. "If you want me, dear, just call."

"Yes, Mummy."

Edmund rapped for attention. Celeste, Frieda, and Theodor glanced around at him. He looked more frightfully strained, they realized, than even they felt. His expression was a study in suppressed excitement, but there were also signs of a knowledge that was almost too overpowering for a human being to bear.

His voice was clipped, rapid. "I think it's about time we stopped worrying about our own affairs and thought of those of the Solar System, partly because I think they have a direct bearing on the disappearances of Ivan and Rosalind. As I told you, I've been sorting out the crucial items from the material we've been presenting. There are roughly four of those items, as I see it. It's rather like a mystery story. I wonder if, hearing those four clues, you will come to the same conclusion I have."

The others nodded.

"First, there are the latest reports from Deep Shaft, which, as you know, has been sunk to investigate deep-Earth conditions. At approximately twenty-nine miles below the surface, the delvers have encountered a metallic obstruction which they have tentatively named the durasphere. It resists their hardest drills, their strongest corrosives. They have extended a side-tunnel at that level for a quarter of a mile. Delicate measurements, made possible by the mirror-smooth metal surface, show that the durasphere has a slight curvature that is almost equal to the curvature of the Earth itself. The suggestion is that deep borings made anywhere in the world would encounter the durasphere at the same depth.

"Second, the movements of the moons of Mars and Jupiter, and particularly the debris left behind

19

by the moons of Mars. Granting Phobos and Deimos had duraspheres proportional in size to that of Earth, then the debris would roughly equal in amount the material in those two duraspheres' rocky envelopes. The suggestion is that the two duraspheres suddenly burst from their envelopes with such titanic velocity as to leave those disrupted envelopes behind."

It was deadly quiet in the committee room.

"Thirdly, the disappearances of Ivan and Rosalind, and especially the baffling hint—from Ivan's message in one case and Rosalind's downward-pointing glove in the other—that they were both somehow drawn into the depths of the Earth.

"Finally, the dreams of the ESPs, which agree overwhelmingly in the following points: A group of beings separate themselves from a godlike and telepathic race because they insist on maintaining a degree of mental privacy. They flee in great boats or ships of some sort. They are pursued on such a scale that there is no hiding place for them anywhere in the universe. In some manner they successfully camouflage their ships. Eons pass and their still-fanatical pursuers do not penetrate their secret. Then, suddenly, they are detected."

Edmund waited. "Do you see what I'm driving at?" he asked hoarsely.

He could tell from their looks that the others did, but couldn't bring themselves to put it into words.

"I suppose it's the time-scale and the value-scale that are so hard for us to accept," he said softly. Much more, even, than the size-scale. The thought that there are creatures in the universe to whom the whole career of Man—in fact, the whole career of life—is no more than a few thousand or hundred thousand years. And to whom Man is no more than a minor stage property—a trifling part of a clever job of camouflage.".

This time he went on, "Fantasy writers have at times hinted all sorts of odd things about the Earth— that it might even be a kind of single living creature, or honeycombed with inhabited caverns, and so on. But I don't know that any of them ever suggested that the Earth, together with all the planets and moons of the Solar System, might be . . ."

In a whisper, Frieda finished for him, ". . . a camouflaged fleet of gigantic spherical spaceships."

"Your guess happens to be the precise truth."

At that familiar, yet dreadly unfamiliar voice, all four of them swung toward the inner door. Dotty was standing there, a sleep-stupefied little girl with a blanket caught up around her and dragging behind. Their own daughter. But in her eyes was a look from which they cringed.

She said, "I am a creature somewhat older than what your geologists call the Archeozoic Era. I am speaking to you through a number of telepathically sensitive individuals among your kind. In each case my thoughts suit themselves to your level of comprehension. I inhabit the disguised and jetless spaceship which is your Earth."

Celeste swayed a step forward. "Baby . . ." she implored.

Dotty went on, without giving her a glance, "It is true that we planted the seeds of life on some of these planets simply as part of our camouflage, just as we gave them a suitable environment for each. And it is true that now we must let most of that life be destroyed. Our hiding place has been discovered,

21

our pursuers are upon us, and we must make one last effort to escape or do battle, since we firmly believe that the principle of mental privacy to which we have devoted our existence is perhaps the greatest good in the whole Universe.

"But it is not true that we look with contempt upon you. Our whole race is deeply devoted to life, wherever it may come into being, and it is our rule never to interfere with its development. That was one of the reasons we made life a part of our camouflage—it would make our pursuers reluctant to examine these planets too closely.

"Yes, we have always cherished you and watched your evolution with interest from our hidden lairs. We may even unconsciously have shaped your development in certain ways, trying constantly to educate you away from war and finally succeeding— which may have given the betraying clue to our pursuers.

"Your planets must be burst asunder—this particular planet in the area of the Pacific—so that we may have our last chance to escape. Even if we did not move, our pursuers would destroy you with us. We cannot invite you inside our ships—not for lack of space, but because you could never survive the vast accelerations to which you would be subjected. You would, you see, need very special accommodations, of which we have enough only for a few.

"Those few we will take with us, as the seed from which a new human race may—if we ourselves somehow survive—be born."

Rosalind and Ivan stared dumbly at each other across the egg-shaped silver room, without apparent

22

entrance or exit, in which they were sprawled. But
their thoughts were no longer of thirty-odd mile
journeys down through solid earth, or of how cool
it was after the heat of the passage, or of how gro-
tesque it was to be trapped here, the fragment of a
marriage. They were both listening to the voice that
spoke inside their minds.

"In a few minutes your bodies will be separated
into layers one atom thick, capable of being shelved
or stored in such a way as to endure almost infinite
accelerations. Single cells will cover acres of space.
But do not be alarmed. The process will be painless
and each particle will be catalogued for future as-
sembly. Your consciousness will endure throughout
the process."

Rosalind looked at her gold-shod toes. She was
wondering, *Will they go first, or my head? Or will I
be peeled like an apple?*

She looked at Ivan and knew he was thinking the
same thing.

Up in the committee room, the other Wolvers
slumped around the table. Only little Dotty sat
straight and staring, speechless and unanswering,
quite beyond their reach, like a telephone off the
hook and with the connection open, but no voice
from the other end.

They had just switched off the TV after listening
to a confused medley of denials, prayers, Kometevskyite chatterings, and a few astonishingly realistic
comments on the possibility of survival.

These last pointed out that, on the side of the
Earth opposite the Pacific, the convulsions would
come slowly when the entombed spaceship burst

forth—provided, as seemed the case, that it moved without jets or reaction.

It would be as if the Earth's vast core simply vanished. Gravity would diminish abruptly to a fraction of its former value. The empty envelope of rock and water and air would begin to escape from the debris because there would no longer be the mass required to hold it.

However, there might be definite chances of temporary and even prolonged survival for individuals in strong, hermetically sealed structures, such as submarines and spaceships. The few spaceships on Earth were reported to have blasted off, or be preparing to leave, with as many passengers as could be carried.

But most persons, apparently, could not contemplate action of any sort. They could only sit and think, like the Wolvers.

A faint smile relaxed Celeste's face. She was thinking, *How beautiful! It means the death of the Solar System, which is a horrifying subjective concept. Objectively, though, it would be a more awesome sight than any human being has ever seen or ever could see. It's an absurd and even brutal thing to wish—but I wish I could see the whole cataclysm from beginning to end. It would make death seem very small, a tiny personal event.*

Dotty's face was losing its blank expression, becoming intent and alarmed.

"We are in contact with our pursuers," she said in the familiar-unfamiliar voice. "Negotiations are now going on. There seems to be—there *is* a change in them. Where they were harsh and vindictive before, they now are gentle and conciliatory." She

24

paused, the alarm on her childish features pinching into anxious uncertainty. "Our pursuers have always been shrewd. The change in them may be false, intended merely to lull us into allowing them to come close enough to destroy us. We must not fall into the trap by growing hopeful . . ."

They leaned forward, clutching hands, watching the little face as though it were a television screen. Celeste had the wild feeling that she was listening to a communique from a war so unthinkably vast and violent, between opponents so astronomically huge and nearly immortal, that she felt like no more than a reasoning amoeba . . . and then realized with an explosive urge to laugh that that was exactly the situation.

"No!" said Dotty. Her eyes began to glow. "They *have* changed! During the eons in which we lay sealed away and hidden from them, knowing nothing of them, they have rebelled against the tyranny of a communal mind to which no thoughts are private . . . the tyranny that we ourselves fled to escape. They come not to destroy us, but to welcome us back to a society that we and they can make truly great!"

Frieda collapsed to a chair, trembling between laughter and hysterical weeping. Theodor looked as blank as Dotty had while waiting for words to speak. Edmund sprang to the picture window, Celeste toward the TV set.

Climbing shakily out of the chair, Frieda stumbled to the picture window and peered out beside Edmund. She saw lights bobbing along the paths with a wild excitement.

On the TV screen, Celeste watched two brightly lit ships spinning in the sky—whether human space-

ships or Phobos and Deimos come to help Earth re-
joice, she couldn't tell.

Dotty spoke again, the joy in her strange voice
forcing them to turn. "And you, dear children, creatures of our camouflage, we welcome you—whatever
your future career on these planets or like ones—into
the society of enlightened worlds! You need not feel
small and alone and helpless ever again, for we shall
always be with you!"

The outer door opened. Ivan and Rosalind reeled
in, drunkenly smiling, arm in arm.

"Like rockets," Rosalind blurted happily. "We
came through the durasphere and solid rock . . .
shot up right to the surface."

"They didn't have to take us along," Ivan added
with a bleary grin. "But you know that already,
don't you? They're too good to let you live in fear,
so they must have told you by now."

"Yes, we know," said Theodor. "They must be almost god-like in their goodness. I feel . . . calm."

Edmund nodded soberly. "Calmer than I ever felt
before. It's knowing, I suppose, that—well, we're
not alone."

Dotty blinked and looked around and smiled at
them all with a wholly little-girl smile.

"Oh, Mummy," she said, and it was impossible to
tell whether she spoke to Frieda or Rosalind or
Celeste, "I've just had the funniest dream."

"No, darling," said Rosalind gently, "it's we who
had the dream. We've just awakened."

THE BIG TREK

I didn't know if I'd got to this crazy place by rocket, space dodger, time twister—or maybe even on foot the way I felt so beat. My memory was gone. When I woke up there was just the desert all around me with the gray sky pressing down like the ceiling of and enormous room. The desert . . . and the big trek. And *that* was enough to make me stop grabbing for my memory and take a quick look at my pants to make sure I was human.

These, well, animals were shuffling along about four abreast in a straggly line that led from one end of nowhere to the other, right past my rocky hole. Wherever they were heading they seemed to have come from everywhere and maybe everywhen. There were big ones and little ones, some like children and some just small. A few went on two feet, but more on six or eight, and there were wrigglers, rollers, oozers, flutterers and hoppers; I couldn't decide whether the low-flying ones were pets or pals. Some had scales, others feathers, bright armor like beetles or fancy hides like zebras, and quite a few wore transparent suits holding air or other gases, or water or other liquids, though some of the suits were tailored for a dozen tenacles and some for no legs at all. And darn if their shuffle—to pick one word for all the kinds of movement—wasn't more like a dance than a lockstep.

They were too different from each other for an army, yet they weren't like refugees either, for refu-

27

gees wouldn't dance and make music, even if on more feet than two or four and with voices and instruments so strange I couldn't tell which was which. Their higgledy-piggledy variety suggested a stampede from some awful disaster or a flight to some ark of survival, but I couldn't feel panic in them—or solemn purpose either, for that matter. They just shuffled happily along. And if they were a circus parade, as a person might think from their being animals and some of them dressed fancy, then who was bossing the show and where were the guards or the audience, except for me?

I should have been afraid of such a horde of monsters, but I wasn't, so I got up from behind the rock I'd been spying over and I took one last look around for footprints or blastscar or time-twister whorls or some sign of how I'd got there, and then I shrugged my shoulders and walked down toward them.

They didn't stop and they didn't run, they didn't shoot and they didn't come out to capture or escort me; they kept on shuffling along without a break in the rhythm, but a thousand calm eyes were turned on me from the tops of weaving stalks or the depths of bony caverns, and as I got close a dusky roller like an escaped tire with green eyes in the unspinning hub speeded up a little and an opal octopus in a neat suit brimful of water held back, making room for me.

Next thing I knew I was restfully shuffling along myself, wondering how the roller kept from tipping and why the octopus moved his legs by threes, and how so many different ways of moving could be harmonized like instruments in a band. Around me was the murmuring rise and fall of languages I

28

couldn't understand and the rainbow-changing of
color patches that might be languages for the eye—
the octopus dressed in water looked from time to
time like a shaken-up pousse-café.

I tried out on them what I seemed to remember
as the lingoes of a dozen planets, but nobody said
anything back at me directly—I almost tried Earth-
talk on them, but something stopped me. A puffy
bird-thing floating along under a gas-bag that was
part of its body settled lightly on my shoulder and
hummed gently in my ear and dropped some sus-
picious-looking black marbles and then bobbed off.
A thing on two legs from somewhere ahead in the
trek waltzed its way to my side and offered me a
broken-edged chunk that was milky with light and
crusty. The thing looked female, being jauntily built
and having a crest of violet feathers, but instead of
nose and mouth her face tapered to a rosy little ring
and where breasts would be there was a burst of pink
petals. I gave my non-Earth lingoes another try. She
waited until I was quiet and then she lifted the
crusty chunk to her rosy ring, which she opened a
little, and then she offered the chunk to me again.
I took it and tasted it and it was like brick cheese
but flaky and I ate it. I nodded and grinned and
she puffed out her petals and traced a circle with
her head and turned to go. I almost said, "Thanks,
chick," because that seemed the right thing, but
again something stopped me.

So the big trek had accepted me, I decided, but
as the day wore on (if they had days here, I reminded myself) the feeling of acceptance didn't
give me any real security. It didn't satisfy me that I
had been given eats instead of being eaten and that

I was part of a harmony instead of a discord. I guess I was expecting too much. Or maybe I was finding a strange part of myself and was frightened of it. And after all it isn't reassuring to shufflle along with intelligent animals you can't talk to, even if they act friendly and dance and sing and now and then thrum strange strings. It didn't calm me to feel that I was someplace that was homey and at the same time as lonely as the stars. The monsters around me got to seem stranger and stranger; I quit seeing their little tricks of personality and saw only their outsides. I craned my neck trying to spot the chick with the pink petals but she was gone. After a while I couldn't bear it any longer. Some ruins looking like chopped off skyscrappers had come in sight earlier and we were just now passing them, not too close, so although the flat sky was getting darker and pressing down lower and although there were distant flashes of lightning and rumbles of thunder (I think that's what they were) I turned at a right angle and walked away fast from the trek.

Nobody stopped me and pretty soon I was hidden in the ruins. They were comforting at first, the little ruins, and I got the feeling my ancestors had built them. But then I came to the bigger ones and they *were* chopped-off skyscrapers and yet some of them were so tall they scratched the dark flat sky and for a moment I thought I heard a distant squeal like chalk on a giant blackboard that set my teeth on edge. And then I got to wondering what had chopped off the skyscrapers and what had happened to the people, and after that I began to see dark things loafing along after me close to the ruined walls. They were about as big as I was, but going on all fours. They began to follow me closer and closer, moving like clumsy wolves, the more notice I took of them. I saw that their faces were covered with hair like their bodies and that their jaws were working. I started to hurry and as soon as I did I began to hear the sounds they were making. The bad thing was that although the sounds were halfway between growls and barks, I could understand them.

"Hello, Joe."

"Whacha know, Joe?"

"That so, Joe?"

"Let's blow, Joe."

"C'mon Joe, let's go, go, go."

And then I realized the big mistake I'd made in coming to these ruins, and I turned around and started to run back the way I had come, and they came loping and lurching after me, trying to drag me down, and the worst thing was that I knew they didn't want to kill me, but just have me get down on all fours and run with them and bark and growl.

The ruins grew smaller, but it was very dark now and at first I was afraid that I had lost my way and next I was afraid that the end of the big trek had passed me by, but then the light brightened under the low sky like the afterglow of a sunset and it showed me the big trek in the distance and I ran toward it and the hairy things stopped skulking behind me.

I didn't hit the same section of the big trek, of course, but one that was enough like it to make me wonder. There was another dusky roller, but with blue eyes and smaller, so that it had to spin faster, and another many-legged creature dressed in water, and a jaunty chick with crimson crest and a burst of orange petals. But the difference didn't bother me.

The trek slowed down, the change in rhythm rippling back to me along the line. I looked ahead and there was a large round hole in the low sky and through it I could see the stars. And through it too the trek itself was swerving, each creature diving upward toward the winking points of light in the blackness.

I kept on shuffling happily forward, though more slowly now, and to either side of the trek I saw heaped on the desert floor spacesuits tailored to fit every shape of creature I could imagine and fly him or her safely through the emptiness above. After a while it got to be my turn and I found a suit and climbed into it and zipped it snug and located the control buttons in the palms of the gloves and looked up. Then I felt more than control buttons in my fingers and I looked to either side of me and I was hand in hand with an octopus wearing an eight-legged spacesuit over his water-filled one and on the other side with a suited-up chick who sported a jet-black crest and pearl-gray petals.

She traced a circle with her head and I did the same, and the octopus traced a smaller circle with a free tenacle, and I knew that one of the reasons I hadn't used Earth-talk was that I was going to keep quiet until I learned or remembered *their* languages, and that another reason was that the hairy four-footers back in the ruins had been men like me and I hated them but these creatures beside me were my kind, and that we had come to take one last look at the Earth that had destroyed itself and at the men who had stayed on Earth and not got away like me—to come back and lose my memory from the shock of being on my degraded ancestral planet.

Then we clasped hands tight, which pushed the buttons in our palms. Our jets blossomed out behind us and we were diving up together out of this world through the smoothly rounded doughnut hole toward the stars. I realized that space wasn't empty and that those points of light in the darkness weren't lonely at all.

THE ENCHANTED FOREST

The darkness was fusty as Formalhautian Aa leaves, acrid as a Rigelian brush fire, and it still shook faintly, like one of the dancing houses of the Wild Ones. It was filled with a petulant, low humming, like nothing so much as a wounded Earth-wasp.

Machinery whirred limpingly, briefly. An oval door opened in the darkness. Soft green light filtered in—and the unique scent, aromatic in this case yet with a grassy sourness, of a new planet.

The green was imparted to the light by the thorny boughs or creepers crisscrossing the doorway. To eyes dreary from deep sub-space the oval of interlaced, wrist-thick tendrils was a throat-lumping sight.

A human hand moved delicately from the darkness toward the green barrier. The finger-long, translucent thorns quivered, curved back ever so slowly, then struck—a hairbreadth short, for the hand had stopped.

The hand did not withdraw but lingered just in range, caressing danger. A sharp gay laugh etched itself against the woundedly-humming dark.

Have to dust those devilish little green daggers to get out of the wreck, Elven thought. *Lucky they were here though. The thorn forest's cushioning-effect may have been the straw that saved the space-boat's back—or at least mine.*

Then Elven stiffened. The humming behind him shaped itself into faint English speech altered by centuries of slurring, but still essentially the same.

"You fly fast, Elven."

"Faster than any of your hunters," Elven agreed softly without looking around, and added, "FTL— meaning Faster Than Light."

"You fly far, Elven. Tens of lightyears," the wounded voice continued.

"Scores," Elven corrected.

"Yet I speak to you, Elven."

"But you don't know where I am. I came on a blind reach through deep sub-space. And your FTL radio can take no fix. You are shouting at infinity, Fedris."

"And fly you ever so fast and far, Elven," the wounded voice persisted, "you must finally go to ground, and then we will search you out."

Again Elven laughed gayly. His eyes were still on the green doorway. "You will search me out! Where will you search me out, Fedris? On which side of the million planets of the sos? On which of the hundred million planets not of the sos?"

The wounded voice grew weaker. "Your home planet is dead, Elven. Of all the Wild Ones, only you slipped through our cordon."

This time Elvne did not comment vocally. He felt at his throat and carefully took from a gleaming locket there a tiny white sphere no bigger than a lady beetle. Holding it treasuringly in his cupped palm, he studied it with a brooding mockery. Then, still handling it as if it were an awesome object, he replaced it in the locket.

The wounded voice had sunk to a ghostly whisper.

"You are alone, Elven. Alone with the mystery and terror of the universe. The unknown will find you, Elven, even before we do. Time and space and fate will all conspire against you. Chance itself will—"

The spectral FTL-radio voice died as the residual power in the wrecked machinery exhausted itself utterly. Silence filled the broken gut of the spaceboat.

Silence that was gayly shattered when Elven laughed a last time. Fedris the Psychologist! Fedris the Fool! Did Fedris think to sap his nerve with witch-doctor threats and the power of suggestion? As if a man—or woman—of the Wild Ones could ever be brought to believe in the supernatural!

Not that there wasn't an unearthliness in the universe, Elven reminded himself somberly—an unearthly beauty born of danger and ultimate self-expression. But only the Wild Ones knew *that* unearthliness. It could never be known to the poor tame hordes of the sos, who would always revere safety and timidity as most members of the human sos—or society—have revered them—and hate all lovers of beauty and danger.

Just as they had hated the Wild Ones and so destroyed them.

All save one.

One, had Fedris said? Elven smiled cryptically, touched the locket at his neck, and leaped lightly to his feet.

A short time later he had what he needed from the wreck.

"And now, Fedris," he murmured, "I have a work of creation to perform." He smiled. "Or should I say recreation?"

He directed at the green doorway the blunt muzzle of a dustgun. There was no sound or flash, but the green boughs shook, blackened—the thorns vanishing—and turned to a drifting powder fine and dark as the ashes carpeting Earth's Moon. Elven sprang to the doorway and for a moment he was poised there, yellow-haired, cool-lipped, laughing-eyed, handsome as a young god—or adolescent devil— in his black tunic embroidered with plati-num. Then he leaned out and directed the dustgun's ultrasonic downward until he had cleared a patch of ground in the thorn forest. When this moment's work was over, he dropped lightly down, the fine dust puffing up to his knees at the impact.

Elven snapped off his dustgun, flirted sweat from his face, laughed at his growing exasperation, and looked around at the thorn forest. It had not changed an iota in the miles he'd made. Just the glassy thorns and the lance-shaped leaves and the boughs rising from the bare, reddish earth. Not another planet to be seen. Nor had he caught the tiniest glimpse of moving life, large or small—save the thorns them-selves, which "noticed" him whenever he came too close. As an experiment he'd let a baby one prick him and it had stung abominably.

Such an environment! What did it suggest, any-how? Cultivation? Or a plant that permeated its environs with poison, as Earth's redwood its woody body. He grinned at the chill that flashed along his spine.

And, if there were no animal life, what the devil were the thorns for?

A ridiculous forest! In its simplicity suggesting the enchanted forests of ancient Earthly fairy tales. That idea should please witch doctor Fedris!

If only he had some notion of the general location

of the planet he was on, he might be able to make better guesses about its other life forms. Life spores did drift about in space, so that solar systems and even star regions tended to have biological similarities. But he'd come too fast and too curiously, too fast even to see stars, in the Wild Ones' fastest and most curious boat, to know where he was.

Or for Fedris to know where he was, he reminded himself.

Or for any deep-space approach-warning system, if there were one on this planet, to have spotted his arrival. For that matter he hadn't foreseen his arrival himself. There had been just the dip up from sub-space, the sinister black confetti of the meteorite swarm, the collision, the wrecked spaceboat's desperate fall, clutching at the nearest planet.

He should be able to judge his location when night came and he could see the stars. That is, if night ever came on this planet. Or if that high fog ever dispersed.

He consulted his compass. The needle of the primitive but useful instrument held true. At least this planet had magnetic poles.

And it probably had night and day, to support vegetable life and such a balmy temperature.

Once he got out of this forest, he'd be able to plan. Just give him cities! One city!

He tucked the compass in his tunic, patting the locket at his neck in a strangely affectionate, almost reverent way.

He looked at the laced boughs ahead. Yes, it was exactly like those fairy forests that cost fairy-book knights so much hackwork with their two-handed swords.

38

Easier with a dustgun—and he had scores of miles of cleared path in his store of ultrasonic refills.

He glanced back at the slightly curving tunnel he'd made.

Through the slaty ashes on its floor, wicked green shoots were already rising.

He snapped on the duster.

The boughs were so thick at its edge that the clearing took Elven by surprise. One moment he was watching a tangled green mat blacken under the duster's invisible beam. The next, he had stepped out—not into fairyland, but into the sort of place where fairy tales were first told.

The clearing was about a half mile in diameter. Round it the thorn forest made a circle. A little stream bubbled out of the poisonous greenery a hundred paces to his right and crossed the clearing through a shallow valley. Beyond the stream rose a small hill.

On the hillside was a ragged cluster of gray buildings. From one of them rose a pencil of smoke. Outside were a couple of carts and some primitive agricultural implements.

Save for the space occupied by the buildings, the valley was under intensive cultivation. The hill was planted at regular intervals with small trees bearing clusters of red and yellow fruit. Elsewhere were rows of bushy plants and fields of grain rippling in the breeze. All vegetation, however, seemed to stop about a yard from the thorn forest.

There was a mournful lowing. Around the hillside came a half dozen cattle. A man in a plain tunic was leisurely driving them toward the buildings. A tiny animal, perhaps a cat, came out of the building with the smoke and walked with the cattle, rubbing against their legs. A young woman came to the door after the cat and stood watching with folded arms.

Elven drank in the atmosphere of peace and rich earth, feeling like a man in an ancient room. Such idyllic scenes as this must have been Earth's in olden times. He felt his taut muscles relaxing.

A second young woman stepped out of a copse of trees just ahead and stood facing him, wide-eyed. She was dressed in a greenish tunic of softened, spun, and woven vegetable fibers. Elven sensed in her a certain charm, half sophisticated, half primitive. She was like one of the girls of the Wild Ones in a rustic play suit. But her face was that of an awestruck child.

He walked toward her through the rustling grain. She dropped to her knees.

"You . . .you—" she murmured with difficulty. Then, more swiftly, in perfect English speech, "Do not harm me, lord. Accept my reverence."

"I will not harm you, if you answer my questions well," Elven replied, accepting the advantage in status he seemed to have been given. "What place is this?"

"It is the Place," she replied simply.

"Yes, but what place?"

"It is the Place," she repeated quakingly. "There are no others."

"Then where did I come from?" he asked.

Her eyes widened a little with terror. "I do not know." She was redhaired and really quite beautiful.

Elven frowned. "What planet is this?"

She looked at him doubtfully. "What is a planet?"

*Perhaps there were going to be language diffi-
culties after all,* Elven thought. "What sun?" he asked.

"What is sun?"

He pointed upward impatiently. "Doesn't that
stuff ever go away?"

"You mean," she faltered fearfully, "does the sky
ever go away?"

"The sky is always the same?"

"Sometimes it brightens. Now comes night."

"How far to the end of the thorn forest?"

"I do not understand." Then her gaze slipped beyond him, to the ragged doorway made by his duster.
Her look of awe was intensified, became touched
with terror. "You have conquered the poison
needles," she whispered. Then she abased herself until her loose, red hair touched the russet shoots of
the grain. "Do not hurt me, all-powerful one," she
gasped.

"I cannot promise that," Elven told her curtly.
"What is your name?"

"Sefora," she whispered.

"Very well, Sefora. Lead me to your people."

She sprang up and fled like a doe back to the
farm buildings.

When Elven reached the roof from which the
smoke rose, taking the leisurely pace befitting his
dignity as god or overlord or whatever the girl had
taken him for, the welcoming committee had already
formed. Two young men bent their knees to him,
and the young woman he had seen standing at the
doorway held out to him a platter of orange and
purple fruit. The Conqueror of the Poison Needles
sampled this refreshment, then waved it aside with

41

a curt nod of approval, although he found it delicious.

When he entered the rude farmhouse he was met by a blushing Sefora who carried cloths and a steaming bowl. She timidly indicated his boots. He showed her the trick of the fastenings and in a few moments he was sprawled on a couch of hides stuffed with aromatic leaves, while she reverently washed his feet.

She was about twenty, he discovered, talking to her idly, not worrying about important information for the moment. Her life was one of farm work and rustic play. One of the young men—Alfors—had recently become her mate.

Outside the gray sky was swiftly darkening. The other young man, whom Elven had first seen driving the cattle and who answered to the name of Kors, now brought armfuls of knotty wood, which he fed to the meager fire, so that it crackled up in rich yellows and reds. While Tuyla—Kor's girl—busied herself nearby with work that involved mouth-watering odors.

The atmosphere was homey, though somewhat stiff. After all, Elven reminded himself, one doesn't have a god to dinner every night. But after a meal of meat stew, fresh-baked bread, fruit conserves, and a thin wine, he smiled his approval and the atmosphere quickly became more celebratory, in fact quite gay. Alfors took a harp strung with gut and sang simple praises of nature, while later Sefora and Tuyla danced. Kors kept the fire roaring and Elven's wine cup full, though once he disappeared for some time, evidently to care for the animals.

Elven brightened. These rustic folk faintly resembled his own Wild Ones. They seemed to have a touch of that reckless, ecstatic spirit so hated by the tame folk of the sos. (Though after a while the resemblance grew too painfully strong, and with an imperious gesture he moderated their gaiety.)

Meanwhile, by observation and questions, he was swiftly learning, though what he learned was astonishing rather than helpful. These four young people were the sole inhabitants of their community. They knew nothing of any culture other than their own.

They had never seen the sun or the stars. Evidently this was a planet whoses axes of rotation and of revolution around its sun were the same, so that the climate was always unvarying at each latitude, the present locality being under a cloud belt. Later he might check this, he told himself, by determining if the days and nights were always of equal length.

Strangest of all, the two couples had never been beyond the clearing. The thorn forest, which they conceived of as extending to infinity, was a barrier beyond their power to break. Fires, they told him, sizzled out against it. It swiftly dulled their sharpest axes. And they had a healthy awe of its diabolically sentient thorns.

All this suggested an obvious line of questioning.

"Where are your parents?" Elven asked Kors.

"Parents?" Kor's brow wrinkled.

"You mean the shining ones?" Tuyla broke in. She looked sad. "They are gone."

"Shining ones?" Elven quizzed. "People like yourselves?"

"Oh no. Beings of metal with wheels for feet and long, clever arms that bent anywhere."

"I have always wished I were made of lovely, bright metal," Sefora commented wistfully, "with wheels instead of ugly feet, and a sweet voice that never changed, and a mind that knew everything and never lost its temper."

Tuyla continued, "They told us when they went why they must go. So that we could live by our own powers alone, as all beings should. But we loved them and have always been sorry."

There was no getting away from it, Elven decided after making some casual use of his special mind-searching powers to test the veracity of their answers. These four people had actually been reared by robots of some sort. But why? A dozen fantastic, unprovable possibilities occurred to him. He remebered what Fedris had said about the mystery of the universe, and smiled wryly.

Then it was his turn to answer questions, hesitant and awestricken ones. He replied simply, "I am a black angel from above. When God created his universe he decided it would be a pretty dull place if there weren't a few souls in it willing to take all risks and dare all dangers. So here and there among his infinite flocks of tame angels, sparingly, he introduced a wild strain, so that there would always be a few souls who would kick up their heels and jump any fences. Yes, and break the fences down too, exposing the tame flocks to night with its unknown beauties and dangers." He smiled around impishly, the firelight making odd highlights on his lips and cheeks. "Just as I've broken down your thorn fence."

It had been pitch black outside for some time. The wine jar was almost empty. Elven yawned. Immediately preparations were made for his rest. The cat got up from the hearth and came and rubbed Elven's legs.

The first pale glow of dawn aroused Elven and he slipped out of bed so quietly that he wakened no one, not even the cat. For a moment he hesitated in the gray room heavy with the smell of embers and the lees of wine. It occurred to him that it would be rather pleasant to live out his life here as a sylvan god adored by nymphs and rustics.

But then his hand touched his throat and he shook his head. This was no place for him to accomplish his mission—for one thing, there weren't enough people. He needed cities. With a last look at his blanket-huddled hostesses and hosts—Sefora's hair had just begun to turn ruddy in the increasing light —he went out.

As he had expected, the thorn forest had long ago repaired the break he had made near the stream. He turned in the opposite direction and skirted the hill until he reached the green wall beyond. There, consulting his compass, he set his course away from the wrecked spaceboat. Then he began to dust.

By early afternoon—judging time from the changing intensity of the light—he made a dozen miles and was thinking that perhaps he should have stayed at the wreck long enough to try to patch up a levitator. If only he could get up a hundred feet to see what—if anything—was going to happen to this ridiculous forest!

For it still fronted him unchangingly, like some wizard growth from a book of fairy tales. The glassy thorns still curved back and struck whenever he swayed too close. And behind him the green shoots still pushed up through the slaty powder.

He thought, what a transition—from ultraphotonic flight in a spaceboat, to this worm's-crawl. Enough to bore a Wild One to desperation, to make him think twice of the simple delights of a life spent as a sylvan god.

But then he unfastened the locket at his throat and took out the tiny white sphere. His smile became an inspired one as he gazed at it gleaming on his palm.

Only one of the Wild Ones had escaped from their beleaguered planet, Fedris had said.

What did Fedris know!

He knew that before Elven reached his spaceboat, he had escaped in disguise through the tremendous cordons of the sos. That in the course of that escape he had twice been searched so thoroughly that it would have been a miracle if he could have concealed more than this one tiny tablet.

But this one tiny tablet was enough.

In it were all the Wild Ones.

Early humans had often been fascinated by the idea of an invisible man. Yet it hadn't occurred to them that the invisible man has always existed, that each one of us begins as an invisible man—the single cell from which each human grows.

Here in this white tablet were the genetic elements of all the Wild Ones, the chromosomes and genes of each individual. Here were fire-eyed Vlana, swashbuckling Nar, softlaughing Forten—they, and a billion others! The identical twins of each last person destroyed with the planet of the Wild Ones, waiting only encasement in suitable denucleated growth cells and nurture in some suitable mother. All rolling prettily in Elven's palm.

So much for the physical inheritance.

And as for the social inheritance, there was Elven.

Then it could all begin again. Once more the Wild Ones could dream their cosmos-storming dreams and face their beautiful dangers. Once more they could seek to create, if they chose, those giant atoms, seeds of new universes, because of which the sos had destroyed them. Back in the Dawn Age physicists had envisioned the single giant atom from which the whole universe had grown, and now it was time to see if more such atoms could be created from energy drawn from sub-space. And who were Fedris and Elven and the sos to say whether or not the new universes might—or should—destroy the old? What matter how the tame herds feared those beautiful, sub-microscopic eggs of creation?

It *must* all begin again, Elven resolved.

Yet it was as much the feel of the thorn shoots rising under his feet, as his mighty resolve, that drove him on.

An hour later his duster disintegrated a tangle of boughs that had only sky behind it. He stepped into a clearing a half mile in diameter. Just ahead a bubbling stream went through a little valley, where russet grain rippled. Beyond the valley was a small, orchard-covered hill. On its hither side, low gray buildings clustered raggedly. From one rose a thread of smoke. A man came around the hill, driving cattle.

Elven's second thought was that something must

have gone wrong with his compass, some force must have been deflecting it steadily, to draw him back in a circle.

His first thought, which he had repressed quickly, had been that here was the mystery Fedris had promised him, something supernatural from the ancient fairy-book world.

And as if time too had been drawn back in a circle—he repressed this notion even more quickly —he saw Sefora standing by the familiar copse of trees just ahead.

Elven called her name and hurried toward her, a little surprised at his pleasure in seeing her again.

She saw him, brought up her hand and swiftly tossed something to him. He started to catch it against his chest, thinking it a gleaming fruit.

He jerked aside barely in time.

It was a gleaming and wickedly heavy-bladed knife.

"Sefora!" he shouted.

The red-haired nymph turned and fled like a doe, screaming, "Alfors! Kors! Tulya!" Elven raced after her.

It was just beyond the first out-building that he ran into the ambush, which seemed to have been organized impromptu in an ancient carpenter's shop. Alfors and Kors came roaring at him from the barn, the one swinging a heavy mallet, the other a long saw. While from the kitchen door, nearer by, Tulya rushed with a cleaver.

Elven caught her wrist and the two of them reeled with the force of her swing. Reluctantly then—hating his action and only obeying necessity—he snatched out his duster for a snap-shot at the nearest of the others.

Kors staggered, lifted his hand to his eyes and brushed away dust. Now Alfors was the closest. Elven could see the inch-long teeth on the twanging, singing saw-blade. Then its gleaming lower length dissolved along with Alfors' hand, while its upper half went screeching past his head.

Kors came on, screaming in pain, swinging the mallet blindly. Elven sent him sprawling with a full-intensity shot that made his chest a small volcano of dust, swung round and cut down Alfors, ducked just in time as the cleaver, transferred to Tulya's other hand, swiped at his neck. They went down together in a heap, the duster at Tulya's throat.

Brushing the fine gray ashes frantically from his face, Elven looked up to see Sefora racing toward him. Her flaming red hair and livid face were preceded by the three gleaming tines of a pitchfork.

"Sefora!" he cried and tried to get up, but Alfors had fallen across his legs. "Sefora!" he cried again imploringly, but she didn't seem to hear him and her face looked only hate, so he snapped on the duster, and tines and face and hair went up in a gray cloud. Her headless body pitched across him with a curious little vault as the blunted pitchfork buried its end in the ground. She hit and rolled over twice. Then everything was very still, until a cow lowed restlessly.

Elven dragged himself from under what remained of Alfors and stood up shakily. He coughed a little, then with a somewhat horrified distaste raced out of the settling gray cloud. As soon as he was in clean air he emptied his lungs several times, shuddered a bit, smiled ruefully at the four motionless forms on which the dust was settling, and set himself to figure things out.

Evidently some magnetic force had deflected his compass needle, causing him to travel in a circle. Perhaps one of the magnetic poles of this planet was in the immediate locality. Of course this was no ordinary polar climate or day-night cycle; still, there was no reason why a planet's axes of magnetism and rotation mightn't be far removed from each other.

The behavior of his last evening's hosts and hostesses was a knottier problem. It seemed incredible that his mere disappearance, even granting they thought him a god, had offended them so that they had become murderous. Ancient Earth-peoples had killed gods and god-symbols, of course, yet that had been a matter of deliberate ritual, not sudden blood-frenzy.

For a moment he found himself wondering if Fedris had somehow poisoned their minds against him, if Fedris possessed some FTL agency that had rendered the whole universe allergic to Elven. But that, he knew, was the merest morbid fancy, a kind of soured humor.

Perhaps his charming rustics had been subject to some kind of cyclic insanity.

He shrugged, then resolutely went into the house and prepared himself a meal. By the time it was ready the sky had darkened. He built a big fire and put in some time constructing out of materials in his pack, a small gyrocompass. He worked with an absent-minded mastery, as one whittles a toy for a child. He noticed the cat watching him from the doorway, but it fled whenever he called to it, and it refused to be lured by the food he set on the hearth. He looked up at the wine jars dangling from the rafters, but did not reach them down.

After a while he disposed himself on the couch Kors and Tulya had occupied the night before. The room grew dim as the fire died down. He succeeded in keeping his thoughts away from what lay outside, except that once or twice his mind pictured the odd little vault Sefora's body had made in pitching over him. In the doorway the cat's eyes gleamed.

When he woke it was full day. He quickly got his things together, adding a little fruit to his pack. The cat shot aside as he went out the door. He did not look at the scene of yesterday's battle. He could hear flies buzzing there. He went over the hill to where he had entered the thorn forest last morning. The thorn trees, with their ridiculous fairy-book persistence, had long ago repaired the opening he'd made. There was no sign of it. He turned on the tiny motor of the gyrocompass, leveled his gun at the green wall, and started dusting.

It was as monotonous a work as ever, but he went about it with a new and almost unsmiling grimness. At regular intervals he consulted the gyrocompass and sighted back carefully along the arrow-straight, shoot-green corridor that narrowed with more than perspective. Odd, the speed with which those thorns grew!

In his mind he rehearsed his long-range course of action. He could count, he must hope, on a generation's freedom from Fedris and the forces of the sos. In that time he must find a large culture, preferably

urban, or one with a large number of the right sort
of domestic animals, and make himself absolute master of it, probably by establishing a new religion.
Then the proper facilities for breeding must be arranged. Next the seeds of the Wild Ones pelleted
in the locket at his throat must be separated—as
many as there were facilities for—and placed in
their living or nonliving mothers. Probably living.
And probably not human—that might present too
many sociological difficulties.

It amused him to think of the Wild Ones reborn
from sheep or goats, or perhaps some wholly alien
rooter or browser, and his mind conjured up a di-
verting picture of himself leading his strange flocks
over hilly pastures, piping like ancient Pan—until
he realized that his mind had pictured Sefora and
Tulya dancing along beside him, and he snapped off
the mental picture with a frown.

Then would come the matter of the rearing and
education of the Wild Ones. His hypothetical community of underlings would take care of the former;
the latter must all proceed from his own brain—sup-
plemented by the library of educational micro-tapes
in the wrecked spaceboat. Robots of some sort would
be an absolute necessity. He remembered the conversation of the night before last, which had indicated that there were or had been robots on this
planet, and lost himself in tenuous speculation—
though not forgetting his gyrocompass observations.

So the day wore on for Elven, walking hour after
hour behind a dustgun into a dustcloud, until he was
almost hypnotized in spite of his self-watchfulness
and a host of disquieting memories fitfully thronged
his mind: the darkness of sub-space; the cat's eyes at

the doorway, the feel of its fur against his ankle; dust billowing from Tulya's throat; the little vault Sefora's body had given in pitching over him, almost as if it rode an invisible wave in the air; an imaginary vision of the blasted planet of the Wild Ones, its dark side aglow with radioactives visible even in deep space; the wasp-like humming in the wrecked spaceboat; Fedris' ghostly whisper, "The unknown will find you, Elven—"

The break in the thorn forest took him by surprise.

He stepped into a clearing half a mile in diameter. Just ahead a stream bubbled through a little valley rippling with russet grain. Beyond was a small, orchard-covered hill against whose side low, gray buildings clustered raggedly. From one rose a ribbon of smoke.

He hardly felt the thorns sting him as he backed into them, though the stimulus they provided was enough to send him forward again a few steps. But such trifles had no effect on the furious working of his mind. He must, he told himself, be up against a force that distorted a gyrocompass as much as a magnet, that even distorted the visual lines of space.

Or else he really was in a fairy-book world where no matter how hard you tried to escape through an enchanted forest, you were always led back at evening to—

He fancied he could see a black cloud of flies hovering near the low gray buildings.

And then he heard a rustling in the copse of trees just ahead and heard a horribly familiar voice call excitedly, "Tulya! Come quickly!"

He began to shake. Then his hair-triggered muscles, obeying some random stimulus, hurled him forward aimlessly, jerked him to a stop as suddenly. Thigh-deep in the grain, he stared around wildly. Then his gaze fixed on a movement in the twilit grain—two trails of movement, shaking the grain but showing nothing more. Two trails of movement working their way from the copse to him.

And then suddenly Sefora and Tulya were upon him, springing from their concealment like mischievous children, their eyes gleaming, their mouths smiling with a wicked delight. Tulya's throat, that he had yesterday seen billow into dust, bulged with laughter. Sefora's red hair, that he had watched puff into a gray cloud, rippled in the breeze.

He tried to run back into the forest but they cut him off and caught him with gales of laughter. At the touch of their hands all strength went out of him, and it seemed to him that his bones were turning to an icy mush as they dragged him along stumblingly through the grain.

"We won't hurt you," Tulya assured him between peals of wicked laughter.

"Oh, Tulya, but he's shy!"

"Something's made him unhappy, Sefora."

"He needs loving, Tulya!" And Elven felt Sefora's cold arms go round his neck and her wet lips press his. Gasping, he tried to push away, and the lips bubbled more laughter. He closed his eyes tight and began to sob.

When next he opened them, he was standing near the gray buildings, and someone had put wreaths of flowers around his neck and smeared fruit on his chin, and Alfors and Kors had come, and all four of

54

them were dancing around him wildly in the twilight, hand in hand, laughing, laughing.

Then Elven laughed too, louder and louder, and their gleaming eyes encouraged him, and he began to spin round and round inside their spinning circle, and they grimaced their joy at his comradeship. And then he raised his dustgun and snapped it on and kept on spinning until the circle of other laughers was only an expanding dust ring. Then, still laughing, he ran over the hill, a cat scampering in swift rushes at his side, until he came to a thorny wall. After his hands and face were puffing with stings, he remembered to lift something he'd been holding in his hand and touch a button on it. Then he marched into a dust cloud, singing.

All night he marched and sang, pausing only to reload the gun with a gleeful automatism, or to take from his pack another flashglobe of cold light, which revealed the small world of green thorns and dust motes around him. Mostly he sang an old Centaurian *lieder* that went:

We'll fall through the stars, my Deborah,
   We'll fall through the skeins of light,
We'll fall out of the Galaxy
   And I'll kiss you again in the night.

Only sometimes he sang "Sefora" instead of "Deborah" and "kill" instead of "kiss." At times it seemed to him that he was followed by prancing goats and sheep and strange monsters that were really his brothers and sisters. And at other times there danced along beside him two nymphs, one red-haired. They sang with him in high sweet voices and smiled at him wickedly. Toward morning he grew tired and unstrapped the pack from his back and threw it away, and later he ripped something from his throat and threw that away, too.

As the sky paled through the boughs, the nymphs and beasts vanished and he remembered that he was someone dangerous and important, and that something quite impossible had truly happened to him. But that if he could really manage to think things through—

The thorn forest ended. He stepped into a clearing a half mile in diameter. Just ahead a stream gurgled through a small valley. Beyond was an orchard-covered hill. Russet grain rippled in the valley. On the hillside low gray buildings clustered raggedly. From one rose a thin streamer of smoke.

And toward him, striding lithely through the grain, came Sefora.

Elven screamed horribly and pointed the dustgun. But the range was too great. Only a ribbon of grain stretching halfway to her went up in dust. She turned and raced toward the buildings. He followed her, gun still pointed and snapped on at full power, running furiously along the dust path, taking wild leaps through the gray clouds.

The dust path drew closer and closer to Sefora until it almost lapped her heels. She darted between two buildings.

Then something tightened like a snake around Elven's knees, and as he pitched forward something else tightened around his upper body, jerking his elbows against his sides. The dustgun flew from his hand as he smashed against the ground.

Then he was lying on his back gasping, and through the thinning dust cloud Alfors and Kors were looking down at him as they wound their lassos tighter and tighter around him, trussing him up. He heard Alfors say, "Are you all right, Sefora?" and a voice reply, "Yes. Let me see him." And then Sefora's face appeared through the dust cloud and looked down into his with cold curiosity, and her red hair touched his cheek, and Elven closed his eyes and screamed many times.

"It was all very simple and there was, of course, absolutely nothing of the supernatural," the Director of Human Research assured Fedris, taking a sip of mellow Magellanic wine from the cup at his elbow. "Elven merely walked in a straight line."

Fedris frowned. He was a small man with a worried look that the most thoroughgoing psychoanalysis had been unable to eradicate. "Of course the Galaxy is tremendously grateful to you for capturing Elven. We never dreamed he'd got as far as the Magellanics. Can't say what horrors we may have escaped—"

"I deserve no credit," the director told him. "It was all sheer accident, and the matter of Elven's nerve cracking. Of course you'd prepared the ground there by hinting to him that the supernatural might take a hand."

"That was the merest empty threat, born of desperation," Fedris interrupted, reddening a bit.

"Still, it prepared the ground. And then Elven had the devilish misfortune of landing right in the middle of our project on Magellanic 47. And that, I admit, might be enough to startle anyone." The director grinned.

Fedris looked up. "Just what is your project? All I know is that it's rather hush-hush."

The director settled back in his easy-chair. "The scientific understanding of human behavior has always presented extraordinary difficulties. Ever since the Dawn Age men have wanted to analyze their social problems in the same way they analyze the problems of physics and chemistry. They've wanted to know exactly what causes produce exactly what results. But one great obstacle has always licked them."

Fedris nodded. "Lack of controls."

"Exactly," the director agreed. "With rats, say, it would be easy. You can have two—or a hundred— families of rats, each family with identical heredity, each in an identical environment. Then you can vary one factor in one family and watch the results. And when you get results you can trust them, because the other family is your control, showing what happens when you don't vary the factor."

Fedris looked at him wonderingly. "Do you mean to say—?"

The director nodded. "On Magellanic 47 we're carrying on that same sort of work, not with rats, but with human beings. The cages are half-mile clearings with identical weather, terrain, plants, animals—everything identical down to the tiniest detail. The bars of the cages are the thorn trees, which our botanists developed specially for the purpose. The inmates of the cages—the human experimental animals—are identical twins—though centuplets would be closer to the right word. Identical upbringing:

58

are assured for each group by the use of robot nurses and mentors, set to perform always the same unvarying routine. These robots are removed when the members of the group are sufficiently mature for our purposes. All our observations are, of course, completely secret—and also intermittent, which had the unfortunate result of letting Elven do some serious damage before he was caught.

"Do you see the setup now? In the thorn forest in which Elven was wrecked there were approximately one hundred identical clearings set at identical intervals. Each clearing looked exactly like the other, and each contained one Sefora, one Tulya, one Alfors, and one Kors. Elven thought he was going in a circle, but actually he was going in a straight line. Each evening it was a different clearing he came to. Each night he met a new Sefora.

"Each group he encountered was identical except for one factor—the factor we were varying—and that had the effect of making it a bit more grisly for him. You see, in those groups we happened to be running an experiment to determine the causes of human behavior patterns toward strangers. We'd made slight variations in their environment and robot-education, with the result that the first group he met was submissive toward strangers; the second was violently hostile; the third as violently friendly; the fourth highly suspicious. Too bad he didn't meet the fourth group first—though, of course, they'd have been unable to manage him except that he was half mad with supernatural terror."

The director finished his wine and smiled at Fedris. "So you see it all *was* the sheerest accident. No one was more surprised than I when, in taking a routine observation, I found that my 'animals' had this gibbering and trussed-up intruder. And you could have knocked me over with a molecule when I found out it was Elven."

Fedris whistled his wonder. "I can sympathize with the poor devil," he said, "and I can understand, too, why your project is hush-hush."

The director nodded. "Yes, experimenting with human beings is a rather hard notion for most people to take. Still it's better than running all mankind as one big experiment without controls. And we're extremely kind to our 'animals'. As soon as our experiment with each is finished, it's our policy to graduate them, with suitable re-education, into the sos."

"Still—" said Fedris doubtfully.

"You think it's a bit like some of the ideas of the Wild Ones?"

"A bit," Fedris admitted.

"Sometimes I think so too," the director admitted with a smile, and poured his guest more wine.

While deep in the thorn forest on Magellanic 47, green shoots and tendrils closed round a locket containing a white tablet, encapsulating all the Wild Ones save Elven in a green and tiny tomb.

DEADLY MOON

Almost a quarter of a million miles above the earth, the moon rode east in her orbit around the larger sphere at the cosmically gentle speed of two-thirds of a mile a second, though to those on the eastward spinning planet below, completing 27 turns for the moon's one, she seemed to move west each night with the stars.

A globe of almost airless, sun-blanched rock two thousand miles wide, Luna hung now beside the earth but moving out beyond her, away from the sun. The only face of her that earthlings ever saw was now half in the full glare of raw sunlight, half in darkness. It was the night of the half moon, or first quarter as it is commonly called.

But on this night of the half moon, Luna at last had two moons of her own, though they were as invisible to earthside viewers as the two tiny moons of Mars. Free-falling around her at almost a mile a second in tight orbits a few score miles above her cratered surface with its "seas" (*mares*) of darker rock, were two small manned ships, one of the American Space Force, one of the Russian Space Force. Making a swift circuit of the moon every two hours, the pilots of these ships were each rushing through independent surveys of the moon's treacherous pumice-powdered surface, in preparation for actual landings of larger exploration ships in the near future.

So more people than ordinarily were looking up

at the moon from earth's evening side. But most of
them were looking up rather more in fear than wonder. The past decade had been one of increasingly
angry bickering between the leaders of the two great
nations. The long-dreaded Third World War seemed
very close and the neck-and-neck race to establish
the first military base on the moon seemed only one
more move bringing it closer.

Nor had the war-heavy atmosphere been im-
proved by the recent suggestion, made almost simultaneously by a Russian scientist and an American
military expert, that the moon would be an ideal
spot for the testing—particularly in deep under-
ground bursts—of atomic bombs, a research activity
theoretically banned on earth itself.

At the moment the Pacific Coast of America was
moving into earth's shadow under the half moon.
The towering evergreen forest on the western slopes
of the Cascade Mountains was dipping and darkening into night.

On a lonely hilltop that lifted out of the forest
toward the center of the state of Washington, not far
east of Puget Sound, two men and a girl were tense-
ly watching the moon "rise"—Luna was already
quite high in the southern sky—over the peaked roof
of a white-walled Cape Cod style home.

The younger man could hardly have been more
than a few years older than the girl—in his mid-
twenties at most—yet he gave the impression of a
matured thoughtfulness and poise. He was dressed
for the city with the conservative elegance of a suc-
cessful professional man.

The older man looked about fifty, though his mustache and eyebrows were still dark and his whole face strongly virile with its deep asymmetric vertical furrows between the brows. His rough sports clothes suited him.

He had an arm clasped around the shoulders of the girl, who likewise was dressed for the country. Her face was beautiful, but now although the evening was chilly, it was beaded with perspiration and it showed the taut, barely controlled terror of a woman who forces herself to watch an excruciating or deadly sight.

"Go on, Janet," the older man prompted harshly. "What does the moon make you think of?"

"A spider," the girl answered instantly. "A bloated white spider hanging just over my head in an invisible web. You see, I have a horror of spiders too, doctor." The last remark she shot as an explanation to the younger man. "Or a revolver! Yes, that's it!— a nickle-plated revolver with mother-of-pearl grips pointed at my chest—pointed at all of us!—by a drooling, giggling old mad-woman whose face is white with powder and whose cheeks have circles of violet rouge and whose yellowed lace dress—"

"I think that's enough demonstration, Professor McNellis," the younger man interrupted. "Now if we could go inside with your daughter—"

"No! I first want to prove to you, Dr. Snowden, that it's only the nightmares that are any real trouble to Janet, that this moon-fear hasn't in any way seriously cracked her waking nerves."

"No, and we don't want it to, either," the younger man retorted quietly.

"Go on, Janet," the older man repeated, ignoring

the implied criticism. "What else do you see in the moon?"

"A man, a rabbit, a clown, a witch, a bat, a beautiful lady," the girl answered in rapid sing-song. She seemed to have lost some of her terror, or at least some of her submissiveness, during the interchange between the two men. She chuckled uneasily and said, "Dad, anyone would think *you* were the psychiatrist, the way you're using the moon for a Rorschach test!" Then her voice went grave with insight. "The moon *is* the original Rorschach inkblot, you know. The *mares* are the faded ink. For thousands of years it's been hanging up there identically the same and people have been seeing things in it. It's the only solid thing you can look at in the heavens that has any shape or parts."

The older man's arm dropped away from the girl a little. "That's quite true," he said in an odd voice. "Yet I never thought of it just that way. In a lifetime of astronomical work I never had just that thought."

The younger man moved in, put his own arm around the girl's shoulders and turned her away from the moon. The older man started to oppose him, then gave way.

"And now, Miss McNellis, since you've made an original contribution to the science of astronomy," the younger man said lightly, "I think that will be enough lunar observation for tonight."

"You're the doctor," the girl told him, managing a little smile. "The Moon Doctor."

"That title's a gross exaggeration, Janet, hung on me by one silly newspaper story," he assured her, smiling back. "Actually I wouldn't go near the place. I'm afraid of space."

"Just the same, Dad got you because you're the Moon Doctor."

"He knows a million times more about the moon than I do. And I'm sure he also knows that it's perfectly normal for a girl whose boyfriend is orbiting around the moon to feel frightened on his account and to view the place he's exploring—or surveying —as an almost supernatural enemy."

"Janet's fear of the moon goes back a lot further than her engagement to Tom Kimbro," the older man put in argumentively.

"Yes, Dad, but I *am* frightened on Tom's account."

"You shouldn't be. Dr. Snowden, I've pointed out to Janet that she's no worse off than a girl engaged to one of the early polar explorers. Better, because polar explorers were away for years."

"Yes, Dad, but their girlfriends couldn't go out in the yard and see Antarctica or the northern icecap hanging in the sky and know that *he* was up there, invisible, but moving across it." The edge-of-hysteria note had returned to her voice and she started slowly to turn around. "I think the moon looks as if it were made of ice," she said with eerie faintness. "Dirty ice with lots of bubbles in it."

"Janet, that's a crackpot theory!" her father said angrily. "How you could even start looking at those *Welt-Eis-Lehre* pamphlets when your father's a legitimate astronomer—"

"It's getting cold out here. We can continue inside," Dr. Andreas Snowden said firmly. This time Professor McNellis did not protest.

The living room was quite livable in spite of the way it was crammed with books and glass-fronted shelves of small meteorites and other items of astro-

nomical interest. After they had settled themselves
and Prof. McNellis had poured coffee at Dr. Snowden's suggestion, the latter fixed the professor's
daughter with a friendly grin for a few moments and
then said, "And now I want to hear all about it,
Janet. Ordinarily I'd talk to you alone, and tomorrow
I will, but this way seems comfortable now. Let's
see, your mother died when you were a little girl and
so you've spent your life with your father, who is a
great student of the moon, although his specialty is
meteorites—and just recently you've become engaged to Lieutenant Commander Tom Kimbro, pilot
and crew of America's first circumlunar survey ship
and infinitely more the Moon Man than I'm the
Moon Doctor."

"I've known Tom for years, though," the girl added, smilingly at ease herself now that there was a
roof overhead. "Dad's always been mixed up in the
Moon Project."

"Yes. Now tell me about this moon-horror of yours.
And please, Prof. McNellis, no professional interrup-
tions no matter what comes up, even Cosmic Ice
Theory."

He said it jokingly, but it sounded like a command
just the same. The professor, less tense now that he
was playing host, took it with good grace.

His daughter glanced gratefully at the young doctor, then grew thoughtful. "The nightmares are the
worst part," she said after a bit. "Especially after
they got so bad two months ago. I'm afraid of going
crazy while I'm having them. In fact, I think I do go
crazy and stay that way for ten minutes or so after
I wake up. That was what happened two months ago
when I reared out of bed and got Dad's revolver

and shot off all the bullets in it through the bedroom window straight at the moon. I knew at the time that it was some sort of gesture I was making—I knew I couldn't hit the moon, or at least I was pretty sure I couldn't—but at the same time I knew it was something I had to do to have my sanity. The only other thing I could have done would have been to dive in our bomb shelter and never come out. You know, it was like when something's broken your nerve and made you cower, and if you don't strike out right away, no matter how convulsively . . ."

"I understand," the doctor said soberly. There was approval in his voice. "Janet what happens in these dreams?"

"Nightmares, you mean. Nightmare, really, for it's always about the same. It repeats." Janet closed her eyes. "Well, I'm standing outside and it's night and then the moon comes across the sky very fast, only it's much bigger and brighter. Sometimes it almost seems to brush the trees. And I squinch down as if it were a big silver express train come out of nowhere behind me and I'm terribly frightened. It plunges out of sight and I think I'm safe, but then it comes roaring up over the opposite horizon, even lower this time. There's a hot smell as if the air were being burnt by friction. This keeps on over and over again, faster and faster, though each time I think it's the last. I begin to feel like Poe's man in 'The Pit and the Pendulum,' tied flat on the floor and looking up at the gleaming pendulum that keeps coming closer each whistling stroke until the knife-edge is about to slice him in two.

"But finally I can't help myself, I get curious. I know it's positively the worst thing I can do, that

67

there's some dreadful law against it, that I'm defying some fantastically powerful authority, but just the same I reach up—don't ask me how I manage when the moon's going so fast, I don't know, and don't ask me how I reach so far when it's still in the tree-tops—sometimes it seems to press its cratered face down into the yard and sometimes I grow an arm long as the magic beanstalk—but anyway I reach up, knowing I shouldn't, and I touch the moon!"

"How does the moon feel to your fingers when you touch it?" Dr. Snowden asked.

"Hairy, like a big spider," Janet answered rapidly. Then she opened her eyes wonderingly. "I never remembered *that* before. The moon is rock. Why did I say it, doctor?"

"I don't know. Forget it." Then, "What happens next?" he asked matter-of-factly.

Janet hugged her elbows and held her knees tight together. "The moon breaks up," she whispered. "It cracks all over like a white plate. For a moment the fragments churn around, then they all come hammering down at me. But in the instant before I'm destroyed and the world with me, while the fragments are still streaking down at me like bullets or an avalanche of rocks or a jack-in-the-box upside down, growing mountain-size in a moment—in that instant I feel this dreadful guilt and I know I'm responsible for it all because I touched the moon. That's when I go crazy." She let out a breath.

Dr. Snowden smiled. "You know, Janet, I can't help thinking how two or three thousand years ago your dream would have been regarded as a clear warning from the gods not to land on the moon—

68

plus a prevision of the dreadful things that would happen to us if we kept on meddling sacrilegiously with the heavenly bodies. *No*, Prof. McNellis, I don't mean a word of that seriously," he added quickly as he noted that the astronomer's expression had become aggressively disapproving. "It's just that I make it a habit at a session like this of saying whatever comes into my head. I believe in bringing even superstitious thoughts out and looking at them. By the way, I'd say Janet's dream shows some elements of Cosmic Ice Theory, wouldn't you? See, I break my own rules as soon as I make them."

"If you dignify it with the name Theory," the professor replied sardonically. "A Viennese engineer named Hoerbiger started the whole *Welt-Eis-Lehre* business—a man with no astronomical training. His weird and wonderful notion was that the moon is made of ice and mud, that it came spiraling in from the infinite and will soon get so close to earth that it will cause floods and earthquakes and then break up, showering us with a fiery frigid hail. What's more, according to Hoerbiger earth has had six previous moons, which all broke up the same way. This one we've got now is the seventh. Incidentally, the break-up of the sixth moon is supposed to have accounted for all legends of universal floods, fire-breathing dragons, falling towers of Babel, the Twilight of the Gods, and what have you.

"It's all nothing new, by the way. In the last century Ignatius Donnelly, who even got to be a member of Congress, wrote it all up in his book *Ragnarok*, except he used comets instead of moons—in those days they thought of comets as more massive. And now Velikovsky's done it again—gone over Hoerbiger once lightly, with comets. Took in some allegedly smart people, too.

"Hoerbiger developed *one* great set of followers at any rate—the Nazis. Most of them were suckers for pseudo-science. Cosmic Ice suited the Nordic superman perfectly.

"Of course, Janet knows all about this—she's read the junk, haven't you, dear?"

The doctor cocked his head and asked quickly, "Am I mistaken, Prof. McNellis, or isn't there nevertheless some shadow of a real scientific theory behind this notion of moons breaking up?"

"Oh yes. If a satellite with a plastic core gets close enough to its mother planet, the tidal action of the latter tears it apart. That's what supposed to have produced the rings of Saturn—the break-up of a moon of Saturn that got too close. The crucial distance is called Roche's limit. In the case of earth it's only six thousand miles above the ground—Luna would have to be that close, even if she had the right kind of core, which she hasn't. It *has* been suggested—by George Gamow—that if everything worked out just right this situation might actually come about—in one hundred billion years!" The professor chuckled. "You can see that none of this stuff applies to our present situation at all."

"Still, it's interesting." The doctor looked back from father to daughter and asked casually, "Janet, do you believe in this *Welt-Eis-Lehre?*"

She shook her head while her father snorted. "But it's interesting," she added with a nervous, almost impish smile.

"I agree," Dr. Snowden said, nodding. "You know,

Hans Schindler Bellamy, Hoerbiger's British disciple, had a very vivid childhood dream almost exactly like yours, that later helped convert him to Hoerbiger."

"Then you already knew what I was telling you about the Cosmic Ice farrago?" Prof. McNellis said accusingly.

"Only a bit here and there," the doctor assured him. "One or two of my patients were converts." He did not pursue the point. "Janet," he said, "I gather your own moon dreams go back to childhood, but they weren't so frightening then?"

"That's right. Except for one time when Dad took me on an ocean cruise just after mother died. I'd see the moonlight dancing on the water. The dreams were very bad then."

Prof. McNellis nodded. "We went to the Caribbean. You were just seven. Almost every night you'd wake up whimpering and blurry-eyed. Naturally, Dr. Snowden, I assumed Janet was reacting to her mother's death."

"Of course. Tell me, Janet, where is the real moon when you have these dreams? I mean, do they tend to cluster around the time of the full moon?"

The girl bobbed her head vigorously. "Once—just once—I remember having the nightmare in the daytime and when I woke up I saw the moon out of the window, faint silver in the pale blue afternoon sky."

Again Prof. McNellis nodded confirmation and said, "For years I've kept a record of Janet's dreams. In every instance the moon was above the horizon when the dream occurred. There were none during the dark of the moon—one of the hundred and seventeen Janet reported to me, at any rate."

The doctor frowned quizzically. "That's a rather

astonishing circumstance, don't you think? To what do you attribute it?"

The professor shrugged. "I don't know. Maybe moonlight is the stimulus that triggers the dream, or was to start with."

"Yes," Janet said rather solemnly. "Doctor, isn't it an old theory that the moon causes mental upsets? You know, Luna and lunacy. And isn't there supposed to be something very special about moonlight? —something affecting growth and women's monthly cycles and the electrical pressures in the blood and the brain?"

"Don't get off on that track, Janet," her father said sharply. "Another real possibility, Dr. Snowden, is that Janet has a moon-clock in her brain and that her subconscious only sends the dream when the moon is topside. I'm just telling you the facts."

Janet raised her hand. "I just remembered," she said excitedly, "that the exact position of the moon in the sky had a lot to with my Caribbean dreams being so bad. Dr. Snowden," she continued anxiously, "you know that up north here the moon is never exactly overhead, that even when it's at its highest in the sky it's still south of the zenith?"

"Yes, I know that much," he grinned.

"Well, when we sailed to the Caribbean I remember Dad explaining to me that now we were in the Tropic Zone the moon could be directly overhead. In fact, on one night of the cruise it *was* directly overhead." She shivered.

"I think I remember telling you about that," her father said, "but I don't recall it making any impression on you at the time. At least you didn't say anything to me."

"I know. I was afraid you'd be angry."

"But why? And why should the moon being in the zenith frighten you especially?"

"Yes, Janet, why?" Dr. Snowden echoed.

She looked back and forth between the two men. "Don't you see? If the moon were straight overhead, it could fall straight down on me. Anywhere else, it might miss me. It's the difference between being in the mouth of a tunnel that may collapse at any minute and being *in* the tunnel."

This time it was the professor who chuckled. "Janet," he said, "you certainly did take this thing seriously when you were a tyke."

"I still take it seriously," she flared at him. "My feelings take it seriously. What holds the moon up? A lot of scientific laws! What if the laws should be repealed, or broken?"

"Oh Janet," was all her father could say, still chuckling, while Dr. Snowden commented, "Your feelings take it seriously—that's a nice phrase, Janet. But your mind doesn't take it seriously, does it?"

"I guess not," she admitted unwillingly.

"For instance," he pressed, "I don't know if it's possible, but suppose there should be a volcanic eruption on the moon, you know that the chunks of rock thrown up would fall back to the moon, don't you? That they couldn't hit the earth? Even if they were shot out toward the earth?"

"I suppose you're right," she agreed after a moment.

"No, you're not, Dr. Snowden—not exactly," Prof. McNellis interjected, getting up. He was grinning with friendly maliciousness. "You say you're a man who believes in speaking his thoughts and settling for nothing less than reality. Good! Those are my own sentiments." He stopped in front of one of the glass-fronted cases. "Come over here, I've got something to show you. You too, Janet—I never told you about these. After your nightmares started, I always believed in playing down the moon to you, until Dr. Snowden convinced me of the superior virtue of always speaking all the truth."

"I didn't exactly say—" Dr. Snowden began and cut himself short. He went over to the case. Janet McNellis stopped just behind him.

Prof. McNellis indicated some specimens of what looked like blackish glass neatly arranged on white cardboard. Most of them seemed to be fragments of small domed disks, but a few were almost perfect buttons a half inch to an inch across.

Prof. McNellis cleared his throat. "Meteorites of this sort are called tektites," he explained. "They are found only in the Tropic Zone or near it—in other words, under the moon. The theory is that when large meteorites hit the moon, some fragments of the moon's siliceous—glassy or sandy—surface are dashed upward at speeds greater than the moon's low escape velocity of a mile and a half a second. Some of these fragments are captured by earth's gravitational field. During their fall to earth they are melted by the heat of friction with the air and take their characteristic button shape. So right here, in all likelihood, you are looking at bits of actual moon-rock, tiny fragments of—*Janet, what is it?*"

Dr. Snowden looked around. Janet was leaning tautly forward, her gaze hypnotically fixed on the tektites. She was trembling visibly. ". . . like spiders," he heard her say faintly.

Suddenly her face convulsed into a mask halfway between panic and rage. She lifted her fists above her head and lunged at the glass. Dr. Snowden grabbed her around the waist, using his other arm to block her descending fists, and in spite of her struggles wrenched her around so that she wasn't looking at the case. She continued to struggle and he could feel her still shivering too.

The professor hesitated, then went out in the hall and called, "Mrs. Pulaski!"

The girl stopped struggling but the doctor didn't release her. "Janet," he whispered sharply, "what do *you* believe causes your dreams?"

"You'll think I'm crazy," she whispered back.

His arms hugged her a little more tightly. "Everyone's crazy," he assured her with great conviction.

"I think my dreams are warnings," she whispered. *"I think they're somehow broadcast to my mind from a station on the moon."*

"Thank you, Janet," the doctor said, releasing her.

Prof. McNellis returned with a stout motherly woman. Janet went to her. " 'Scuse me, everybody, I was goofy," she said. "G'night, Dad, doctor."

When the two women were gone the two men looked at each other. The doctor lifted his empty coffee cup. As the professor poured for both of them, he said ruefully, "I guess I was the goofy one, shocking Janet that way."

"It's almost impossible to tell in advance how something like that will work out," the doctor consoled him. "Though I'll admit I was startled by those tektites myself. I'd never heard of the things."

The professor frowned. "There are a lot of things

about the moon that most people don't know. But what do you think about Janet?

"It's too soon to say. Except that she seems remarkably stable, both mentally and emotionally, for whatever it is she's going through."

"I'm glad to hear you say that."

"You mustn't worry about her cracking up, professor, but I also advise you not to put her in any more test situations."

"I won't!—I think I've learned my lesson." The professor's tone grew confidential. "Dr. Snowden, I've often wondered if some childhood trauma mayn't have been the cause of Janet's moon-dread. Perhaps she believed that my interest in astronomy —to a child, the moon—was somehow responsible for her mother's death."

"Could be," the doctor nodded thoughtfully. "But I have a hunch that the real cause of Janet's dreams has nothing to do with psychoanalysis or *Welt-Eis-Lehre* or her anxiety about Tom Kimbro."

The professor looked up. "What else then?" he asked sharply.

The doctor shrugged. "Again it's too early to say."

The professor studied him. "Tell me," he said, "why are you called the Moon Doctor? The Moon Project recommended you—I didn't investigate any further."

"I had luck treating a couple of Project executives who had nervous breakdowns—but that isn't the main reason." The doctor held out his cup for more coffee. After taking a swallow, he began, "I had a run of private patients who had a horror of the moon mixed up with their troubles. It seemed too much

76

of a coincidence, so I sent out feelers and inquiries to other psychiatrists, lay analysts, mental hospitals, psycho wards, and so on. The answers came in fast! —evidently there were dozens of doctors as puzzled as I. It turned out that there were literally thousands of cases of mental aberration characterized by moon-dread, hundreds of them involving dreams very similar to Janet's about the moon breaking up—exploding, suffering giant volcanic eruptions, colliding with a comet or with earth itself, cracking under tidal strain, and so on."

The professor shook his head wonderingly. "I knew Project Moon had touched off a bit of a panic reaction, but I never dreamed it went that deep."

The doctor said, "In hundreds of cases—again like Janet's—there was a history of mild moon-fears going back to childhood."

"Hmm—sounds like the onset of the mass neurosis, or whatever you'd call it, coincided with the beginnings of high rocketry and space travel."

"Apparently. But then how do you explain this? For about four thousand dreams of moon break-up I got dates—day, hour, approximate minute. In ninety seven percent of those instances the moon was above the horizon when the dream occurred. I've become convinced that some straight-line influence traveling from the moon to the dreamer is at work—something that, like short radio waves, can be blocked off by the curve and mass of the earth."

"Moonlight?" the professor suggested quickly.

"No. These dreams occur just as often when the local sky is heavily clouded as when it's clear. I don't think light or any other part of the electromagnetic spectrum is responsible. I think it's an entirely different order of waves."

The professor frowned. "Surely you're not suggesting something like thought-waves? You know, doctor, even if there is such a thing as telepathy or extrasensory perception, the chances are it takes place instantaneously, altogether outside the world of space and time. The notion of thought-waves similar to those of light and sound is primitive."

"I don't know," the doctor said. "Galileo thought that *light* moved instantaneously too, but it turned out that it was just too fast for him to measure. The same might be true of thought-waves—that they go much faster than light, that they *seem* to move instantaneously. But only seem—another century may refine techniques for measuring their speed."

"But Einstein—" The professor shrugged. "In any case the notion of telepathy is completely hypothetical."

"I don't know," the doctor repeated. "While you were calling the nurse, Janet quieted and I took the opportunity to ask her what she thought was causing her dreams. She said, '*I think my dreams are broadcast to my mind from a station on the moon.*' Prof. McNellis, that is by no means the first time a patient with moon-horror has made that suggestion to me."

The professor bowed his head, massaging his brow as if it were beginning to ache. "I guess I don't know either," he muttered.

The doctor's eyes brightened. "But perhaps you do," he said softly. He leaned forward. "Professor McNellis," he continued, "what is it that's really happening on the moon? What is it that you Project people have been observing on the moon's surface

78

that you won't reveal to outsiders, not even to me? What is it that Tom Kimbro may be glimpsing now?"

The professor didn't look up, but his hand stopped massaging his forehead.

"Professor McNellis, I *know* you've been observing something strange on the moon. I got unmistakable hints of it from one of my Project patients, but even in his condition he let himself be gagged by security regulations. What is it? You don't suppose I came way out here *only* to treat Janet, do you?"

For several seconds neither man moved or spoke. It was a contest of wills. Then the professor looked up shiftly.

"For centuries some astronomers, usually the less dependable ones, have been observing all sorts of 'strange' things on the moon," he began evasively. "One hundred and fifty years ago Gruithuisen reported seeing a fortress near the crater Schroeter. One hundred years ago Zentmayer saw mountain-size objects marching or moving across the moon during an eclipse. Bright spots have been seen, black spots, spots like giant bats—Charles Fort's books of newspaper-science are crammed with examples! Really, Dr. Snowden, strange things seen on the moon are an old, many-times-exploded story." His voice had grown loud and assertive, but he did not meet the doctor's eyes.

"Professor McNellis, I'm not interested in past observations of strange appearances on the moon," the doctor pressed on insistently. "What I want to know is what's being observed on the moon right now. It's my guess that it has nothing to do with Russian activities—I've heard through European colleagues that there's been a sizable outbreak of some kind of moon-psychosis, plus moon-dreams, in the Soviet Union too—so you don't have *that* reason for making security regulations sacrosanct. Please tell me, Professor McNellis—I need the information if I'm to treat Janet successfully."

The professor twisted in his chair, finally and miserably, "It's been made top secret. They're mortally afraid of setting off a major panic, or having the whole Project canceled."

"Professor McNellis, a panic *is* being set off and maybe the Project *should* be canceled, but that's nothing to me. My interest is solely professional— my own profession."

"Even when you were recommended to me as a psychiatrist, I was warned against telling you about the observations. And if Janet ever heard a word of them, she *would* go mad."

"Professor McNellis, I'm a grown man. I'm reasonably responsible. I may need that information to save your daughter's sanity."

The professor looked up hollow-eyed, at last meeting the doctor's gaze. "I'll chance it," he said. "Two months ago our moon telescope in the 24-hour-satellite, where the seeing isn't blurred by atmosphere, began to observe activity of an unknown nature in four separate areas of the moon: near Mare Nectaris, in Mare Foecunditatis, north of Mare Crisium, and in the moon's very center by Sinus Medii. It was impossible to determine the nature of the activity. At first we thought it was the Russians secretly got there ahead of us, but Space Intelligence disposed of that possibility. The observations themselves mounted simply to a limited and variable darkening in the four areas—shadows, you might say, though one viewer described what he saw as 'towers, some moving.'

"Then two days ago the survey went into orbit—purposely on orbit that would take it over Nectaris and Foecunditatis. On his first pass Tom Kimbro reported glimpsing at both sites—here I quote him verbatim—*spiderlike or skeletal machines, towering thin creatures not men, and evidence of deep shafts being dug.*"

The professor jerked to his feet. "That's all," he said with a rapid shrug. "Since that first report, the Project's cut me off from information too. Whatever else Tom's seen—either confirming or negating those first glimpses—and whatever's happened to him, I haven't been told."

The hall door opened. "Professor McNellis," Mrs. Pulaski said, "isn't Janet here? She said she wanted to speak to you, but the outside door's open."

The professor looked guilt-struck at the doctor. "Do you suppose she was listening from the hall? That she heard me?" The doctor was already moving past Mrs. Pulaski.

He spotted Janet at once. Her quilted silk dressing gown stood out like white paint. She was standing in the center of the lawn, looking up over the roof.

Motioning Mrs. Pulaski back and gripping the professor's arm for silence, he moved out beside the girl.

She did not seem to notice their approach. Her lips were working a little. Her thumbs kept lightly rubbing her fingertips. Her gaze, wide-eyed, staring, was fixed on the moon.

The doctor knew that his first concern should be

for his patient, but now he realized that, even before that, he too must look at the moon.

Half black and merged with space, half faintly mottled white, Luna hung starkly, her glow blanking out all but the most brilliant nearby stars. She looked smaller to the doctor than he'd been thinking of her. He realized, with irrelevant guilt, that although he'd been thinking a lot about the moon in the past two years, he hadn't bothered to look at her often and certainly hadn't studied her.

"The four sites?" he heard himself ask softly.

"Three of them are near the curving outer edge of the illuminated half," the professor answered as quietly. "The fourth is right in the middle of the shadow line."

Janet did not appear to hear them. Then, with no more warning than a gasp of indrawn breath, she screamed.

The doctor shot his arm around her shoulders, but he did not take his gaze off the moon.

Two seconds passed. Perhaps three. The moon did not change.

Then, by the curving edge, he thought he saw three tiny smudges. He asked himself what they could be at a quarter of a million miles. Giant cracks many miles across? Huge sections lifting? He blinked his eyes to clear them.

Then he was looking at the violet stars. There were four of them, brighter than Venus, although three were in the illuminated half disk at the same spots where he'd seen the smudges. The fourth, brightest of all, was dead center, bisecting the straight boundary between the bright and dark halves of the disk.

He kept looking—it would have been completely beyond his power not to—but the psychiatrist-section of his mind, operating independently, made him say loudly, "I'm seeing it too, Janet! We're all seeing it. It's real!" He said that more than once, gripping her shoulders tightly each time he spoke.

He heard Professor McNellis croak, "Ten seconds," and realized he must mean the time since the smudges appeared.

The violet stars were growing less glitteringly bright and at the same time they were expanding. They became violet balls or round spots, still brighter than the moon, but paling, as big at the moment as pingpong balls if you thought of the moon as a basketball, but they were growing.

"Explosion fronts," the professor whispered, continuing at intervals to croak the time.

Two of the spots, near the edge, overlapped without losing their perfect circularity. The central spot was still brightest, especially where it expanded into the dark half. The spots were big as tennis balls now, big as baseballs.

"Atomic charges. Have to be. Huge beyond imagining. Set *hundreds* of miles deep." The professor was still speaking in a whisper.

The doctor found he was hunching his shoulders in expectation of a shattering blast, then remembered there was no air to carry sound from the moon. Some day he must ask the professor how long it would take sound to get from the moon to the earth if there *were* air to carry it. He glanced at

Janet and at the same moment she looked around at him questioningly. He simply nodded once, then they both looked up again.

The four spots all overlapped now, each grown to half the moon's diameter, and they were getting hard to see against the bright half—just a thin violet wash edged with deeper violet. Soon they were indistinguishable except for the one spreading from the moon's center across the dark side. For an eerie moment it outlined the dark edge of the moon with a violet semi-circle, then vanished too.

"One minute," croaked the professor. "Blast-front speed 17 miles a second."

Where the first smudges and violet stars had been were now four dark marks, almost black. The central one was hardest to see—a jag in the shadow line. They were just large enough to show irregular edges to keen eyes.

"Blast holes. One hundred, two hundred miles across. As deep, probably deeper." The professor maintained his commentary.

Then they saw the chunks.

The ones blasted from the Crisium and Foecunditatis holes were already clear of the side of the moon and gleaming with reflected sunlight themselves. Three were large enough to show their jagged shape.

"The biggest. One twentieth moon diameter by eye. One hundred miles across. Big as the asteroid Juno. New Hampshire cubed."

It almost seemed possible to see the movement of the chunks. The doctor finally decided he couldn't quite. It was like trying to see the movement of the minute hand of a watch. Yet every time he blinked and looked back, they seemed to have fanned out a little farther.

"Four minutes."

It became clear that the chunks were moving at different apparent speeds. The doctor decided it might be because they had been thrown up at different angles. He wondered why he so wanted to keep watching them—perhaps so as not to think about them? He glanced at Janet. She seemed to be watching them with an almost relaxed interest. He probably need worry no more about her mind. Now that her fears had become something real and shared, she would hardly aberrate. No neuroses in wartime. One thing seemed likely about Janet, though—that she'd sensed the explosions telepathically. She'd screamed two or three seconds before he'd seen anything, and it takes light a second and a half to make the moon-earth trip.

There were some lights gleaming now on the dark side of the moon, near its center, one of them large enough to have an irregular appearance. Those must be chunks from Sinus Medii, the doctor told himself. He shivered.

The fastest moving Crisium chunks were now the moon's own width beyond the side of the moon.

"Eight minutes."

The professor's voice was almost normal again, though still hushed, as he calculated aloud, "One moon diameter in eight minutes. Round off to two thousand miles in five hundred seconds. Gives a chunk velocity of four miles a second. Needn't worry about the stuff from Crisium, Foecunditatis, even

Nectaris. Won't come anywhere near us—miss earth by hundreds of thousands of miles. But the chunks from Medii are headed *here,* or near here. Starting near moon escape speed of a mile and a half a second it would take the chunks four days for the trip. But starting at around four miles a second, figure about one day. Yes, those Medii chunks should near-miss or hit us in about 24 hours—or at least close enough to that time so that we'll be on the impact side of earth."

When he finished he was no longer talking to himself and for the first time since the catastrophe began he had taken his eyes off the moon and was looking at his daughter and the doctor.

That he should be doing so was nothing exceptional. All over earth's evening side people who had been looking up in the sky were now looking around at each other.

The British Isles and West Africa missed the sight. There the moon, setting around midnight, had been down for a good hour.

In Asia and most of the Soviet Union it was day.

But all the Western Hemisphere—all the Americas —had a clear view of it.

The first conspicuous consequence was the rumor, traveling like a prairie fire, that the communist Russians were testing planet-killer bombs on the moon, or that World War Three had already started there. This rumor persisted long after Conelrad was on the air and the National Disaster Plan in effect. In the Eastern Hemisphere it metamorphosed into the rumor that the capitalist Americans, ever careless of the safety of the human race and invariably wasteful of natural resources, were ravishing Luna, ruining earth's only moon to satisfy the lusts of mad stock-brokers and insane artillery generals.

Less conspicuously, but quite as swiftly, the tele-scopes of the west began to sort out the Sinus Medii chunks and make preliminary estimates of their in-dividual trajectories. Organized amateur meteor watchers rendered significant aid, particularly in keeping up to date, minute by minute, the map of the expanding chunk-jumble.

Very fortunately for the world, clear weather pre-vailed, cloud-cover everywhere was at a minimum—though in any case clouds could not have interfered with probably the most important telescope involved —that on the 24-hour satellite hanging 22,100 miles above the Pacific Ocean south of Mexico.

First observations added up to this: headed to-ward earth was a jumble of chunks ranging down in size from a planetoid ninety miles in diameter, a dozen fragments ten or more miles across, some three score of mass of the order of one cubic mile, and presumably any number of smaller chunks plus a thin cloud of moon-gravel and dust. They would reach the immediate vicinity of earth in almost exactly one day, conforming remarkably to Professor McNellis' rough estimate. Those that entered earth's atmosphere would do so at a speed low for meteor-ites, yet high enough to burn up the very smallest and to ensure that the large chunks, little slowed by the air because of their great mass relative to cross-section would strike the ground or the seas with im-pact speeds around six miles a second. The strike would be almost completely confined to the Western Hemisphere, clustering around the 120th meridian.

As soon as this last item of news was released, transocean airlines were besieged by persons loaded with money for tickets and bribes, and many did escape to the other side of the earth before most commercial planes were gone or grounded. Meanwhile numerous private planes took off on fantastically perilous transocean flights.

It was good that the telescopes of the Americas got to work swiftly. In six hours the earth's rotation had carried them out of sight of the moon and the Sinus swarm. First the Soviets and Asia, then Europe and Africa, moved into night and had their view of catastrophe hurtling down.

By that time the chunks from the three explosion sites on the moon's western rim had moved out far enough to be almost inconspicuous among the stars. But the Sinus swarm, steadily growing in apparent size and gradually fanning out, presented a brilliant spectacle, those against the dark half of the moon pocking it with points of light, those against the bright half more difficult to see but the largest visible as dark specks, while those that had fanned out most made a twinkling halo around Luna.

Asian and Russian, then European and African telescopes took up the task of charting chunk trajectories, ably supplementing the invaluable work of the moon 'scope in the 24-hour satellite, which kept up a steady flow of observation except for the two hours earth's intervening bulk cut it off from sight of the Sinus swarm. The satellite 'scope was especially helpful because, observing at radio-synchronized times in tandem with an earth 'scope, it was able to provide triangulations on a base some 25,000 miles long.

With incredulous shivers of relief it gradually became apparent that the 90-mile planetoid and many of the other large members of the swarm were going to shoot past earth on the side away from the sun. At first they had seemed to be the ones most on target, but since at a right angle to their explosion-velocity they all also had the moon's own orbital velocity of two-thirds of a mile a second, they drifted steadily east. A few might ruffle the top of the atmosphere, glowing in their passage, and all of them would go into long narrow elliptical orbits around earth, some of them perhaps slowing and falling in the far future, but that was now of less than no consequence.

It was in the chunks that had seemed sure to miss earth widely to the west that the danger lay. For these inevitably drifted east too—onto target.

With maddening but unavoidable delays the major bullseye chunks were sorted out and their points of impact approximated, approximated more narrowly, and finally pin-pointed. Once given, an evacuation order cannot be effectively rescinded, and an error of twenty miles in calculated point of impact would mean many evacuees fleeing to certain death.

By nightfall in London it was clear that a plus-ten-mile-diameter chunk would hit somewhere in the South Pacific and a plus-one-mile chunk in the American northwest or British Columbia.

These two chunks were of special interest because they were the ones that the Russians and American moon-survey ships elected to ride down last.

Both survey ships had the good fortune to escape the blasts, and both had large fuel reserves since it had originally been planned that each should shift orbits several times during the survey. As soon as they became aware of the blasts and their effects each pilot independently decided that his greatest usefulness lay in matching trajectories with the Sinus swarm and riding it down to earth. Accordingly they broke out of their circumlunar orbits and blasted toward the twinkling jumble of moon-rock between them and the gleaming skyblue semicircle of earth, for them in half phase. As soon as, risking collisions with tailenders, they were able to report that they had caught up with the swarm, their radio signals were of unique service in determining the trajectory of the swarm, supplementing telescopic observations.

But the self-imposed task of the survey ships was to become even more perilous. By exactly matching trajectories with a large chunk—a matter largely of eyework and finicky correction blasts—and then holding that course for a matter of minutes, the survey ship's radio signals, gave earth stations an exact fix on that chunk and its course, though at first there were confusions as to *which* chunk, judging by 'scope, the survey ship was matching trajectories with. Thereafter it was for the pilots a matter of blasting gingerly over to the next major chunk, risking collision with minor fragments every second, and matching trajectories with *that*.

In its final trajectory-matching, the Russian ship satisfied earth stations that the plus-ten-mile chunk would land in the open Pacific midway between Baja California and Easter Island and between the Galapagos and Marquises. Warnings of giant waves had already gone out to the Pacific islands and coastal areas, but were now followed up with more specific alarms.

Immediately thereafter the Russian ship went out of radio contact 30,000 miles above the equator, possibly broached by one or more chunks while blasting sideways into a circumterran orbit. Its exact fate as a piece of matter was never known, but its performance was enshrined in men's hearts and helped raise the framework of the International Meteor Guard.

Twenty-two minutes later the 24-hour satellite had its own "curtain raising" encounter with the western edge of the swarm. It was twice holed, but its suited-up personnel effected repairs. A radarman was killed and the moon 'scope smashed.

Meanwhile both Americas had an unequalled sight of the Sinus swarm as earth's own shadow line moved from Recife to Quito and on from Halifax to Portland. As it approached its "comfortable" 15,000-mile miss of earth, the 90-mile "Vermont-cubed" chunk attained the apparent size of the moon—a jagged moon, shaped like a stone arrowhead. Fierce soot-painted Indians discharged barbed arrows back at it from the banks of the Orinco, while at Walpi and Oraibi white-masked Hopi kachinas danced on imperturbably hour after hour.

Everywhere in the United States families sat outdoors or in their cars, listening to Conelrad, ready to move if advised. Already some were filing out like dispossessed ants from known danger points, crowding highways and railways, jamming the insides and clinging to the outsides of coaches, buses, and private cars, many simply legging it with their portable radios murmuring—most refugees tried to follow the insistently repeated advice from Conelrad to "keep listening for further possible revisions in your local impact points."

In a few cities there was a fairly orderly movement into bomb shelters. Stampedes, riots, and other disturbances were surprisingly few—the amazing spectacle in the night sky appeared to have an inhibiting effect.

Bizarre reactions occurred scatteredly. Some splinter religious and cultist groups gathered on hilltops to observe God's judgment on Sodom and Gomorrah. Others did the same thing simply for kicks, generally with the assistance of alcohol. A Greenwich Village group conducted solemn rooftop rites to propitiate the Triple Goddess in her role of Diana the Destroyer.

During the last hour several airports were invaded by survival-gangs and mobs convinced that only persons in the air when the swarm struck would survive the shock of the impact, and a few overloaded planes, some commandeered, took off laboredly or crashed in the attempt.

Tom Kimbro rode the U.S. survey ship down along the final course of the plus-one-mile chunk, keeping about a quarter mile west of its raw gray side. While his ranging radio pulsed signals, he spoke a message over the voice circuit: "Ship's losing air. Must have sprung a seam on the last bump. But I'm safe in my suit. As I came from behind the moon on my last circuit, heading for the shadow line and Nectaris and just before I spotted the violet front and the Sinus chunks rising south, I think I saw *their* ships blasting away from the sun. There were five of them

—skeletal ships—I could see the stars through them
—with barely visible greenish jets. They set off those
blasts like you'd set off firecrackers to scare dogs.
I don't know. Give my love to Janet."

Immediately after that he successfully swung west
into a braking orbit and brought down the ship safely next day on the Utah salt flats. His final trajectory-
matching had helped pinpoint the exact spot near
the center of the state of Washington where the Big
Chunk would land.

The moon is made of rock that averages out a little
more than three times as heavy as water. The Big
Chunk had a mass of rather more than a thousand
million tons. Its impact at almost six miles a second
would release raw energy equivalent to about 1500
nominal atomic bombs (Hiroshima type), nothing
unimaginable in an era of fusion bombs. There
would not be the initial chromatic electromagnetic
flash (heat, light, gamma rays) of an atomic weapon. A typical mushroom cloud would be raised, but
the fallout would be clean, lacking radioactives. The
blast wave would be the same, the earth shock
heavier.

The Big Chunk would be only one of several almost as large hitting the Western Hemisphere along
with almost countless other moon meteorites, many
of them large enough to produce impact energy in
the atomic-bomb range.

As the Sinus swarm traveled the last few hundred
miles to impact or by-pass, gleaming with reflected
sunlight in earth's night sky like so many newborn
stars, a few showing jagged shapes, there was a
breathtaking transformation. Beginning (for North
American viewers) with those to the south, but rap-

idly traveling north across the sky, the lights of the Sinus swarm winked out as the chunks plunged into earth's shadow. To watchers it was as if the chunks had vanished. Some persons fell on their knees and gave thanks, believing that they had witnessed a miracle—a last-minute divine intervention. Then, again starting toward the south, dark red sparks began to glow almost where the Sinus lights had been and in the same general pattern, as the chunks entered the atmosphere and were heated toward incandescence by friction with air molecules.

Beginning in southern California, but swiftly fanning out north and east, every state in the Union had its own Great Sinus Shower. Dazzling ribbons and trails, ionization glows, heat glows, strange radio hissings and roars that came from the ground itself (energized by massive radio emanations from chunk trails in the ionosphere), explosions in the air as a few shunks tortured by heat blew apart, then the walloping deafening blast waves of the impacts, meteor-booms as their roar of passages finally caught up with the chunks, dust clouds spurting up to blanket the stars, wildly eddying winds, re-echoing reverberations.

Then, at last, silence.

Every state in the Union had its casualties, heroisms, and freaks. Seven hundred deaths were subsequently verified, grimly settling once and for all the niggling old dispute as to whether a human being had ever really been killed by a meteorite and it was assumed that at least three hundred more perished unrecorded. The city of Globe, Arizona, was destroyed by a direct hit after a commendably orderly and thorough evacuation. Three telephone girls at a town near Emporia, Kansas, and four radarmen at an early warning station north of Milwaukee stayed phoning Get-Out warnings and making last-minute observations until it was too late to escape physically from their point-of-impact posts. The inhabitants of a Saskatchewan village took a road 9 to death instead of a road 5 to safety, victims of someone's slovenly articulation. A Douglas DC-9 was struck and smashed in midair. A strike in the Texas Panhandle released a gusher of oil. A 25-square-block slum on Chicago's south side, long slated for clearance, was razed meteoritically.

Except within miles of major impact points, ground shock was surprisingly slight, less than that of a major earthquake, seismograph recordings nowhere indicating energy releases higher than 5 on Richter's logarithmic scale.

The giant waves did not quite live up to expectations either and although according to some calculations the Pacific Chunk should have raised the water level of earth's oceans by four hundredths of an inch, this increase was never verified by subsequent measurement. Nor was any island of moon rock miles high created in the Pacific—only the Sinus Shoal, formed by the break-up of the Pacific Chunk on impact and the distribution of its fragments across the bottom. At the time of the impact several fishing boats, private yachts, and one small steamer were never heard from again and presumably engulfed. Another steamer had its back broken by the first giant surge and sank, but its crew successfully abandoned ship and survived to a man, as did three persons on a balsa raft. These last claimed afterwards to have seen the Pacific Chunk at close range "hanging in the sky like a redhot mountain." Hours later, California, Mexican, and South American beaches were impressively slopped over and there was some loss of life in the Hawaiian Islands, though the inhabitants of the 50th state were by then far more interested in the volcanic eruption that had been touched off by the odd chance of a sizable moon-chunk falling into one of the craters of the volcano Mauna Loa.

Alaska, eastern Siberia, and most of the Pacific Islands reported daytime meteor roars and some scattered impacts—including the spectacular spray plumes of ocean strikes—while by an almost amusing coincidence the widely separated cities of Canberra, Yokohama, and the town of Ikhotsk were each simultaneously terrorized by a daytime meteor that glowed and roared miles (some said yards!) above the rooftops and then reportedly departed into space again without striking anywhere.

Janet McNellis, her father, and Dr. Snowden rode out the Washington blast with no great discomfort in the Professor's bomb shelter, though the doctor always afterwards looked a bit sourly at people who spoke of the "trivial" earthquake effects of the Great Sinus Shower. By dawn the dust had cleared sufficiently, the great mushroom cloud blowing away east, so that they had a clear view from their hilltop of a considerable segment of the blast area, on the margin of which they had survived.

The house behind them had its walls and roof buckled somewhat, but had not collapsed. The glass had been blown out of all the windows, although they had been left open before impact. Everywhere the white paint was smoothly shaded with green, as though by a giant airbrush—the great fist of the blast wave had worn a green glove of leaves and pine needles.

The naked trees from which the latter had been stripped marched disconsolately down the hillside. About a mile away these standing wooden skeletons began to give way to a limitless plain of bare-trunked fallen trees that the blast had combed as neatly as straight hair. As one studied them it became apparent that the fallen trunks radiated out from a blast center beyond the horizon and some fifteen miles away.

"Precisely like Kulik's photographs of the impact site of the Great Siberian Meteor of 1908!" Professor McNellis commented.

Janet sighed and snuggled her coat a little more warmly around her. "You know," she remarked, "I don't think I'm going to have any more moon nightmares."

"I don't imagine you will," Dr. Snowden said carefully. "Earth has now received the warning of which your telepathic dreams, and those of many others, were a prevision."

"You think they really were telepathic?" she asked half skeptically.

He nodded.

"But *why* a warning?" the professor demanded. "Why *such* a warning? Why not at least talk to us first?"

He seemed to be asking the questions more of the bare treetrunks than of his daughter or the doctor; nevertheless the latter ventured a speculative answer.

"Maybe *they* don't think we're worth talking to, only worth scaring. I don't know. Maybe they *did* talk to us—maybe that's what the dreams were. They might be a telepathic race, you know, and assume the same means of communication in others. Maybe they only set off their intimidation-blasts after we didn't answer them, or seemed to answer insanely."

"Still, *such* a warning."

The doctor shrugged. "Perhaps they thought it was exactly what we deserve. After all, we must seem a menacing species in some respects—reaching out for the stars when we're still uncertain as to whether it wouldn't be best for one half of our race to destroy the other half." He sighed. "On the other hand," he said, "maybe some of the creatures with whom we share the universe are simply not sane by their standards. Maybe if we knew all we could know about them with our limited minds, we'd still judge them maniacs. I don't know. What we do know now is something we should have known all the time: that we're not the only inhabitants of the galaxy and obviously not—yet—the most powerful!"

THE SNOWBANK ORBIT

The pole stars of the other planets cluster around Polaris and Octans, but Uranus spins on a snobbishly different axis between Aldebaran and Antares. The Bull is her coronet and the Scorpion her footstool. Dear blowzy old bitch-planet, swollen and pale and cold, mad with your Shakespearean moons, white-mottled as death from Venerean Plague, spinning on your side like a poisoned pregnant cockroach, rolling around the sun like a fat drunken floozie with green hair rolling on the black floor of an infinite barroom, what a sweet last view of the Solar System you are for a cleancut young spaceman . . .

Grunfeld chopped off that train of thought short. He was young and the First Interstellar War had snatched him up and now it was going to pitch him and twenty other Joes out of the System on a fast curve breaking around Uranus—and so what! He shivered to get a little heat and then applied himself to the occulted star he was tracking through *Prospero's* bridge telescope. The star was a twentieth planetary diameter into Uranus, the crosslines showed—a glint almost lost in pale green. That meant its light was bulleting 1600 miles deep through the seventh planet's thick hydrogen atmosphere, unless he were seeing the star on a mirage trajectory—and at least its depth agreed with the time since rim contact.

At 2000 miles he lost it. That should mean 2000 miles plus of hydrogen soup above the methane ocean, an America-wide layer of gaseous gunk for the captain to play the mad hero in with the fleet.

Grunfeld didn't think the captain wanted to play the mad hero. The captain hadn't gone space-simple in any obvious way like Croker and Ness. And he wasn't, like Jackson, a telepathy-racked visionary entranced by the Enemy. Worry and responsibility had turned the captain's face into a skull which floated in Grunfeld's imagination when he wasn't actually seeing it, but the tired eyes deep-sunk in the dark sockets were still cool and perhaps sane. But because of the worry the captain always wanted to have the last bit of fact bearing on the least likely maneuver, and two pieces of evidence were better than one. Grunfeld found the next sizable star due to occult. Five-six minutes to rim contact. He floated back a foot from the telescope, stretching out his thin body in the plane of the ecliptic—strange how he automatically assumed that orientation in free fall! He blinked and blinked, then rested his eyes on the same planet he'd been straining them on.

The pale greenish bulk of Uranus was centered in the big bridge spaceshield against the black velvet dark and bayonet-bright stars, a water-splotched and faded chartreuse tennis ball on the diamond-spiked bed of night. At eight million miles she looked half the width of Luna seen from Earth. Her whitish equatorial bands went from bottom to top, where Grunfeld knew, they were spinning out of sight a three miles a second—a gelid waterfall that he imagined tugging at him with ghostly geen gangrenous fingers and pulling him over into a hydrogen Niagara

Half as wide as Luna. But in a day she'd overflow the port as they whipped past her on a new miss an in another day she'd be as small as this again, but behind them, sunward, having altered their outward course by some small and as yet unpredictable angle, but no more able to slow *Prospero* and her sister ships or turn them back at their 100 miles a second than the fleet's solar jet could operate at this chilly distance from Sol. G'by, fleet. G'by, C.C.Y. space-man.

Grunfeld looked for the pale planet's moons. Miranda and Umbriel were too tiny to make disks, but he distinguished Ariel four diameters above the planet and Oberon a dozen below. Spectral sequins. If the fleet were going to get a radio signal from any of them, it would have to be Titania, occulted now by the planet and the noisy natural static of her roiling hydrogen air and seething methane seas—but it had always been only a faint hope that there were survivors from the First Uranus Expedition.

Grunfeld relaxed his neck and let his gaze drift down across the curving star-bordered forward edge of *Prospero's* huge mirror and the thin jutting beams of the pot lattice arm to the dim red-lit gages below the spaceshield.

Forward Skin Temperature seven degrees Kelvin. Almost low enough for helium to crawl, if you had some helium. *Prospero's* insulation, originally designed to hold out solar heat, was doing a fair job in reverse.

Aft (sunward) Skin Temperature 75 degrees Kelvin. Close to that of Uranus' sunlit face. Check.

Cabin Temperature 43 degrees Fahrenheit. Brr! The Captain was a miser with the chem fuel remaining. And rightly . . . if it were right to drag out life

as long as possible in the empty icebox beyond
Uranus.

Gravities of Acceleration zero. Many other zeros.

The four telltales for the fleet unblinkingly glowed
dimmest blue—one each for *Caliban, Snug, Moth,*
and *Starveling,* following *Prospero* in the astern on
slave automatic—though for months inertia had
done all five ships' piloting. Once the buttons had
been green, but they'd wiped that color off the
boards because of the Enemy.

The gages still showed their last maximums. Skin
793 Kelvin, Cabin 144 Fahrenheit, Gravs 3.2. All of
them hit almost a year ago, when they'd been ace-
ing past the sun. Grunfeld's gaze edged back to the
five bulbous pressure suits, once more rigidly upright
in their braced racks, that they'd been wearing during that stretch of acceleration inside the orbit of
Mercury. He started. For a moment he'd thought he
saw the dark-circled eyes of the captain peering between two of the bulging black suits. Nerves! The
captain had to be in his cabin, readying alternate piloting programs for Copperhead.

Suddenly Grunfeld jerked his face back toward
the spaceshield—so violently that his body began
very slowly to spin in the opposite direction. This
time he'd thought he saw the Enemy's green flashing
near the margin of the planet—bright green, viridian,
far vivider than that of Uranus herself. He drew himself to the telescope and feverishly studied the area
Nothing at all. Nerves again. If the Enemy were
much nearer than a light-minute, Jackson would esp
it and give warning. The next star was still three
minutes from rim contact. Grunfeld's mind retreated

to the circumstances that had brought *Prospero* (then only *Mercury One*) out here.

II

When the First Interstellar War erupted, the pioneer fleets of Earth's nations had barely pushed their explorations beyond the orbit of Saturn. Except for the vessels of the International Meteor Guard, space-flight was still a military enterprise of America, Russia, England and the other mega-powers.

During the first months the advantage lay wholly with the slim black cruisers of the Enemy, who had an antigravity which allowed them to hover near planets without going into orbit; and a frightening degree of control over light itself. Indeed, their principal weapon was a tight beam of visible light, a dense photonic stiletto with an effective range of several Jupiter-diameters in vacuum. They also used visible light, in the green band, for communication as men use radio, sometimes broadcasting it and sometimes beaming it loosely in strange abstract pictures that seemed part of their language. Their gravity-immune ships moved by reaction to phototonic jets the tightness of which rendered them invisible except near the sun, where they tended to ionize electronically dirty volumes of space. It was probably this effective invisibility, based on light-control, which allowed them to penetrate the Solar System as deep as Earth's orbit undetected, rather than any power of travel in time or sub-space, as was first assumed. Earthmen could only guess at the physical appearance of the Enemy, since no prisoners were taken on either side.

Despite his impressive maneuverability and armament, the Enemy was oddly timid about attacking live planets. He showed no fear of the big gas planets, in fact hovering very close to their turgid surfaces, as if having some way of fueling from them.

Near Terra the first tactic of the black cruisers, after destroying Lunostrovok and Circumluna, was to hover behind the moon, as though sharing its tide-lockedness—a circumstance that led to a sortie by Earth's Combined Fleet, England and Sweden excepted.

At the wholly disastrous Battle of the Far Side, which was visible in part to naked-eye viewers on Earth, the Combined Fleet was annihilated. No Enemy ship was captured, boarded, or seriously damaged—except for one which, apparently by a fluke, was struck by a fission-headed anti-missile and proceded after the blast to "burn," meaning that it suffered a slow and puzzling disintegration, accompanied by a dazzling rainbow display of visible radiation. This was before the "stupidity" of the Enemy with regard to small atomic missiles was noted, or their allergy to certain radio wave bands and also before Terran telepaths began to claim cloudy contact with Enemy minds.

Following Far Side, the Enemy burst into activity, harrying Terran spacecraft as far as Mercury and Saturn, though still showing great caution in maneuver and making no direct attacks on planets. It was as if a race of heavily armed marine creatures should sink all ocean-going ships or drive them to harbor, but make no assaults beyond the shore line. For a full year Earth, though her groundside and satellite rocketyards were furiously busy, had no vehicle in deep space—with one exception.

At the onset of the War a fleet of five mobile bases of the U. S. Space Force were in orbit to Mercury, where it was intended they take up satellite positions prior to the prospecting and mineral exploitation of the small sun-blasted planet. These five ships, each with a skeleton five-man crew, were essentially Ross-Smith space stations with a solar drive, assembled in space and intended solely for space-to-space flight inside Earth's orbit. A huge paraboloid mirror, its diameter four times the length of the ship's hull, superheated at its focus the hydrogen which was ejected as a plasma at high exhaust velocity. Each ship likewise mounted versatile radio-radar equipment on dual lattice arms and carried as ship's launch a two-man chemical fuel rocket adaptable as a fusion-headed torpedo.

After Far Side, this "tin can" fleet was ordered to bypass Mercury and, tacking on the sun, shape an orbit for Uranus, chiefly because that remote planet, making its 84-year circuit of Sol, was currently on the opposite side of the sun to the four inner planets and the two nearer gas giants Jupiter and Saturn. In the empty regions of space the relatively defenseless fleet might escape the attention of the Enemy.

However, while still accelerating into the sun for maximum boost, the fleet received information that two Enemy cruisers were in pursuit. The five ships cracked on all possible speed, drawing on the solar drive's high efficiency near the sun and expending all their hydrogen and most material capable of being vaporized, including some of the light-metal hydrogen storage tanks—like an old steamer burning her cabin furniture and the cabins themselves to win a race. Gradually the curving course that would have taken years to reach the outer planet flattened into a hyperbola that would make the journey in 200 days.

In the asteroid belt the pursuing cruisers turned aside to join in the crucial Battle of the Trojans with Earth's largely new-built, more heavily and wisely armed Combined Fleet—a battle that proved to be only a prelude to the decisive Battle of Jupiter.

Meanwhile the five-ship fleet sped onward, its solar drive quite useless in this twilight region even if it could have scraped together the needed boilable ejectant mass to slow its flight. Weeks became months. The ships were renamed for the planet they were aimed at. At least the fleet's trajectory had been truly set.

Almost on collision course it neared Uranus, a mystery-cored ball of frigid gas 32,000 miles wide coasting through space across the fleet's course at a lazy four miles a second. At this time the fleet was traveling at 100 miles a second. Beyond Uranus lay only the interstellar night, into which the fleet would inevitably vanish . . .

Unless, Grunfeld told himself . . . unless the fleet shed its velocity by ramming the gaseous bulk of Uranus. This idea of atmospheric braking on a grand scale had sounded possible at first suggestion, half a year ago—a little like a man falling off a mountain or from a plane and saving his life by dropping into a great thickness of feathery new-fallen snow.

Supposing her solar jet worked out here and she had the reaction mass, *Prospero* could have shed her present velocity in five hours, decelerating at a comfortable one G.

But allowing her 12,000 miles of straight-line travel through Uranus' frigid soupy atmosphere—and that might be dipping very close to the methane seas blanketing the planet's hypothetical mineral core—*Prospero* would have two minutes in which to shed her velocity.

Two minutes—at 150 Gs.

Men had stood 40 and 50 Gs for a fractional second.

But for two minutes . . . Grunfeld told himself that the only surer way to die would be to run into a section of the Enemy fleet. According to one calculation the ship's skin would melt by heat of friction in 90 seconds, despite the low temperature of the abrading atmosphere.

The star Grunfeld had been waiting for touched the hazy rim of Uranus. He drifted back to the eyepiece and began to follow it in as the pale planet's hydrogen muted its diamond brilliance.

III

In the aft cabin, lank hairy-wristed Croker pinned another blanket around black Jackson as the latter shivered in his trance. Then Croker turned on a small light at the head of the hammock.

"Captain won't like that," plump pale Ness observed tranquilly from where he floated in womb position across the cabin. "Enemy can feel a candle of *our* light, captain says, ten million miles away." He rocked his elbows for warmth and his body wobbled in reaction like a pollywog's.

"And Jackson hears the Enemy think . . . and Heimdall hears the grass grow," Croker commented with a harsh manic laugh. "Isn't an Enemy for a billion miles, Ness." He launched aft from the hammock. "We haven't spotted their green since Saturn orbit. There's nowhere for them."

"There's the far side of Uranus," Ness pointed out. "That's less than ten million miles now. Eight. A bare day. They could be there."

"Yes, waiting to bushwack us as we whip past on our way to eternity," Croker chuckled as he crumpled up against the aft port, shedding momentum. "That's likely, isn't it, when they didn't have time for us back in the Belt?" He scowled at the tiny white sun, no bigger a disk than Venus, but still with one hundred times as much light as the full moon pouring from it—too much light to look at comfortably. He began to button the inner cover over the port.

"Don't do that," Ness objected without conviction. "There's not much heat in it but there's some." He hugged his elbows and shivered. "I don't remember being warm since Mars orbit."

"The sun gets on my nerves," Croker said. "It's like looking at an arc light through a pinhole. It's like a high, high jail light in a cold concrete yard. The stars are highlights on the barbed wire." He continued to button out the sun.

"You ever in jail?" Ness asked. Croker grinned.

With the tropism of a fish, Ness began to paddle

108

toward the little light at the head of Jackson's hammock, flicking his hands from the wrists like flippers. "I got one thing against the sun," he said quietly. "It's blanketing out the radio. I'd like us to get one more message from Earth. We haven't tried rigging our mirror to catch radio waves. I'd like to hear how we won the battle of Jupiter."

"If we won it," Croker said.

"Our telescopes show no more green around Jove," Ness reminded him. "We counted 27 rainbows on Enemy cruisers 'burning.' Captain verified the count."

"Repeat: if we won it." Croker pushed off and drifted back toward the hammock. "If there was a real victory message they'd push it through, even if the sun's in the way and it takes three hours to catch us. People who win, shout."

Ness shrugged as he paddled. "One way or the other, we should be getting the news from Titania station," he said. "They'll have heard."

"If they're still alive and there ever was a Titania Station," Croker amended, backing air violently to stop himself as he neared the hammock. "Look, Ness, we know that the First Uranus Expedition arrived. At least they set off their flares. But that was three years before the War and we haven't any idea of what's happened to them since and if they ever managed to set up housekeeping on Titania—or Ariel or Oberon or even Miranda or Umbriel. At least if they built a station could raise Earth I haven't been told. Sure thing *Prospero* hasn't heard anything . . . and we're getting close."

"I won't argue," Ness said. "Even if we raise 'em, it'll just be hello-goodby with maybe time between for a battle report."

"And a football score and a short letter from home, ten seconds per man as the station fades." Croker frowned and added, "If Captain had cottoned to my idea, two of us at any rate could have got off this express train at Uranus."

"Tell me how," Ness asked drily.

"How? Why, one of the ship's launches. Replace the fusion-head with the cabin. Put all the chem fuel in the tanks instead of divvying it between the ship and the launch."

"I haven't got the brain for math Copperhead has, but I can subtract," Ness said, referring to *Prospero's* piloting robot. "Fully fueled, one of the launches has a max velocity change in free-fall of 30 miles per second. Use it all in braking and you've only taken 30 from 100. The launch is still going past Uranus and out of the system at 70 miles a second."

"You didn't hear all my idea," Croker said. "You put piggyback tanks on your launch and top them off with the fuel from the other four launches. Then you've 100 miles of braking *and* a maneuvering reserve. You only need to shed 90 miles, anyway. Ten miles a second's the close circum-Uranian velocity. Go into circum-Uranian orbit and wait for Titania to send their jeep to pick you up. Have to start the maneuver four hours this side of Uranus, though. Take that long at 1 G to shed it."

"Cute," Ness conceded. "Especially the jeep. But I'm glad just the same we've got 70 per cent of our chem fuel in our ships' tanks instead of the launches. We're on such a bull's eye course for Uranus—Copperhead really pulled a miracle plotting our orbit—that we may need a sidewise shove to miss her. If we slapped into that cold hydrogen soup at our 100 mps—"

Croker shrugged. "We still could have dropped a couple of us," he said.

"Captain's got to look after the whole fleet," Ness said. "You're beginning to agitate, Croker, like you was Grunfeld—or the captain himself."

"But if Titania Station's alive, a couple of men dropped off would do the fleet some good. Stir Titania up to punch a message through to Earth and get a really high-speed retrieve-and-rescue ship started out after us. *If* we've won the War."

"But Titania Station's dead or never was, not to mention its jeep. And we've lost the Battle of Jupiter. You said so yourself," Ness asserted owlishly. "Captain's got to look after the whole fleet."

"Yeah, so he kills himself fretting and the rest of us die of old age in the outskirts of the Solar System. Join the Space Force and See the Stars! Ness, do you know how long it'd take us to reach the nearest star —except we aren't headed for her—at our 100 mps? Eight thousand years!"

"That's a lot of time to kill," Ness said. "Let's play chess."

Jackson sighed and they both looked quickly at the dark unlined face above the cocoon, but the lips did not flutter again, or the eyelids. Croker said, "Suppose he knows what the Enemy looks like?"

"I suppose," Ness said. "When he talks about them it's as if he was their interpreter. How about the chess?"

"Suits. Knight to King Bishop Three."

"Hmm. Knight to King Knight Two, Third Floor."

"Hey, I meant flat chess, not three-D," Croker objected.

"That thin old game? Why, I no sooner start to get the position really visualized in my head than the game's over."

"I don't want to start a game of three-D with Uranus only 18 hours away."

Jackson stirred in his hammock. His lips worked. "They . . ." he breathed. Croker and Ness instantly watched him. "They . . ."

"I wonder if he is really inside the Enemy's mind?" Ness said.

"He thinks he speaks for them," Croker replied and the next instant felt a warning touch on his arm and looked sideways and saw dark-circled eyes in a skull-angular face under a battered cap with a tarnished sunburst. Damn, thought Croker, how does the captain always know when Jackson's going to talk?

"They are waiting for us on the other side of Uranus," Jackson breathed. His lips trembled into a smile and his voice grew a little louder, though his eyes stayed shut. "They're welcoming us, they're our brothers." The smile died. "But they know they got to kill us, they know we got to die."

The hammock with its tight-swathed form began to move past. Croker and he snatched at it. The captain had pushed off from him for the hatch leading forward.

Grunfeld was losing the new star at 2200 miles into Uranus when he saw the two viridian flares flashing between it and the rim. Each flash was circled by a fleeting bright green ring, like a mist halo. He thought he'd be afraid when he saw that green again, but what he felt was a jolt of excitement that made him grin. With it came a touch on his shoulder. He thought, the captain always knows.

"Ambush," he said. "At least two cruisers."

He yielded the eyepiece to the captain. Even without the telescope he could see those incredibly brilliant green flickers. He asked himself if the Enemy was already gunning for the fleet through Uranus.

The blue telltales for *Caliban* and *Starveling* began to blink.

"They've seen it too," the captain said. He snatched up the mike and his next words rang through the *Prospero*.

"Rig ship for the snowbank orbit! Snowbank orbit with stinger! Mr. Grunfeld, raise the fleet.

Aft, Croker muttered, "Rig our shrouds, don't he mean? Rig shrouds and firecrackers mounted on Fourth of July rockets."

Ness said, "Cheer up. Even the longest strategic withdrawal in history has to end some time."

IV

Three quarters of day later Grunfeld felt a spasm of futile fear and revolt as the pressure suit closed like a thick-fleshed carnivorous plant on his drugged and tired body. Relax, he told himself. Fine thing if you cooked up a fuss when even Croker didn't. He though of forty things to recheck. Relax, he repeated —the work's over; all that matters is in Copperhead's memory tanks now, or will be as soon as the captain's suited up.

The suit held Grunfled erect, his arms at his sides —the best attitude, except he was still facing forward, for taking high G, providing the ship herself didn't start to tumble. Only the cheekpieces and visor hadn't closed in on his face—translucent hand-thick petals as yet unfolded. He felt the delicate firm pressure of built-in fingertips monitoring his pulses and against his buttocks the cold smooth muzzles of the jet hypodermics that would feed him metronomic drugs during the high-G stretch and stimulants when they were in free-fall again. When.

He could swing his head and eyes just enough to make out the suits of Croker and Ness to either side of him and their profiles wavy through the jutting misty cheekpieces. Ahead to the left was Jackson— just the back of his suit, like a black snowman standing at attention, pale-olive-edged by the great glow of Uranus. And to the right the captain, his legs suited but his upper body still bent out to the side as he checked the monitor of his suit with its glowing blue button and the manual controls that would lie under his hands during the maneuver.

Beyond the captain was the spaceshield, the lower quarter of it still blackness and stars, but the upper three-quarters filled with the onrushing planet's pale mottled green that now had the dulled richness of watered silk. They were so close that the rim hardly showed curvature. The atmosphere must have steep gradient, Grunfeld thought, or they'd already be feeling decel. That stuff ahead looked more like water than any kind of air. It bothered him that the captain was still half out of his suit.

There should be action and shouted commands, Grunfeld thought, to fill up these last tight-stretched minutes. Last orders to the fleet, port covers being cranked shut, someone doing a countdown on the firing of their torpedo. But the last message had gone to the fleet minutes ago. Its robot pilots were set to follow *Prospero* and imitate, nothing else. And all the rest was up to Copperhead. Still . . .

Grunfeld wet his lips. "Captain," he said hesitantly. "Captain?"

"Thank you, Grunfeld." He caught the edge of the skull's answering grin. "We are beginning to hit hydrogen," the quiet voice went on. "Forward skin temperature's up to 9 K."

Beyond the friendly skull, a great patch of the rim of Uranus flared bright green. As if that final stimulus had been needed, Jackson began to talk dreamily from his suit.

"They're still welcoming us and grieving for us. I begin to get it a little more now. Their ship's one thing and they're another. Their ship is frightened to death of us. It hates us and the only thing it knows to do is to kill us. They can't stop it, they're even less than passengers . . ."

The captain was in his suit now. Grunfeld sensed a faint throbbing and felt a rush of cold air. The cabin refrigeration system had started up, carrying cabin heat to the lattice arms. Intended to protect them from solar heat, it would now do what it could against the heat of friction.

The straight edge of Uranus was getting hazier. Even the fainter stars shone through, spangling it. A bell jangled and the pale green segment narrowed as the steel meteor panels began to close in front of the spaceshield. Soon there was only a narrow vertical ribbon of green—*bright* green as it narrowed to a thread—then for a few seconds only blackness except for the dim red and blue beads and semi-circles, just beyond the captain, of the board. Then the muted interior cabin lights glowed on.

Jackson droned: They and their ships come from very far away, from the edge. If this is the continuum, they come from the . . . discontinuum, where they don't have stars but something else and where gravity is different. Their ships came from the edge on a gust of fear with the other ships, and our brothers came with it though they didn't want to . . ."

And now Grunfeld thought he began to feel it— the first faint thrill, less than a cobweb's tug, of *weight*.

The cabin wall moved sideways. Grunfeld's suit had begun to revolve slowly on a vertical axis.

For a moment he glimpsed Jackson's dark profile —all five suits were revolving in their framework. They locked into position when the men in them were facing aft. Now at least retinas wouldn't pull forward at high-G decel, or spines crush through thorax and abdomen.

The cabin air was cold on Grunfeld's forehead. And now he was sure he felt weight—maybe five pounds of it. Suddenly aft was *up*. It was as if he were lying on his back on the spaceshield.

A sudden snarling roar came through his suit from the beams bracing it. He lost weight, then regained it and a little more besides. He realized it was their torpedo taking off, to skim by Uranus in the top of the atmosphere and then curve inward the little their chem fuel would let them, homing toward the En emy. He imaged its tiny red jet over the great gray-green glowing plain. Four more would be taking off from the other ships—the fleet's feeble sting. Like a bee's, just one, in dying.

The cheekpieces and foreheadpiece of Grunfeld's suit began to close on his face like layers of pliable ice.

Jackson called faintly, "*Now* I understand. Their ship—" His voice was cut off.

Grunfeld's ice-mask was tight shut. He felt a small surge of vigor as the suit took over his breathing and sent his lungs a high-oxy air. Then came a tingling numbness as the suit field went on, adding an extra prop against decel to each molecule of his body.

But the weight was growing. He was on the moon now . . . now on Mars . . . now back on Earth . . .

The weight was stifling now, crushing—a hill of invisible sand. Grunfeld saw a black pillow hanging in the cabin above him aft. It had red fringe around it. It grew.

There was a whistling and shaking. Everything lurched torturingly, the ship's jets roared, everything recovered, or didn't.

The black pillow came down on him, crushing out sight, crushing out thought.

The universe was a black tingling, a limitless ache floating in a large black infinity. Something drew back and there was a dry fiery wind on numb humps and ridges—the cabin air on his face, Grunfeld decided, then shivered and started at the thought that he was alive and in freefall. His body didn't feel like a mass of internal hemorrhages. Or did it?

He spun slowly. It stopped. Dizziness? Or the

117

suits revolving forward again? If they'd actually come through—

There was a creaking and cracking. The ship contracting after frictional heating?

There was a faint stink like ammonia and formaldehyde mixed. A few Uranian molecules forced past plates racked by turbulence?

He saw dim red specks. The board? Or last flickers from ruined retinas? A bell jangled. He waited, but he saw nothing. Blind? Or the meteor guard jammed? No wonder if it were. No wonder if the cabin lights were broken.

The hot air that had dried his sweaty face rushed down the front of his body. Needles of pain pierced him as he slumped forward out of the top of his opening suit.

Then he saw the horizontal band of stars outlining the top of the spaceshield and below it the great field of inky black, barely convex upward. *That must,* he realized, *be the dark side of Uranus.*

Pain ignored, Grunfeld pushed himself forward out of his suit and pulled himself past the captain's to the spaceshield.

The view stayed the same, though broadening out: stars above, a curve-edged velvet black plain below. They were orbiting.

A pulsing, color-changing glow from somewhere showed him twisted stumps of the radio lattices. There was no sign of the mirror at all. It must have been torn away, or vaporized completely, in the fiery turbulence of decel.

New Maxs showed on the board: Cabin Temperature 214 F, Skin Temperature 907 K, Gravs 87.

Then in the top of the spacefield, almost out of vision, Grunfeld saw the source of the pushing glow: two sharp-ended ovals flickering brightly all colors against the pale starfields, like two dead fish phosphorescing.

"The torps go to 'em," Croker said, pushed forward beside Grunfeld to the right.

"I did find out at the end," Jackson said quietly from the left, his voice at last free of the trance-tone. "The Enemy ships weren't ships at all. They were (there's no other word for it) space animals. We've always thought life was a prerogative of planets, that space was inorganic. But you can walk miles through the desert or sail leagues through the sea before you notice life and I guess space is the same. Anyway the Enemy was (what else can I call 'em?) space-whales. Inertialess space-whales from the discontinuum. Space-whales that ate hydrogen (that's the only way I know to say it) and spat light to move and fight. The ones I talked to, our brothers, were just their parasites."

"That's crazy," Grunfeld said. "All of it. A child's picture."

"Sure it is," Jackson agreed.

From beyond Jackson, Ness, punching buttons, said, "Quiet."

The radio came on thin and wailing with static: "Titania Station calling fleet. We have jeep and can orbit in to you. The *two* Enemy are dead—the last in the System. Titania Station calling fleet. We have jeep fueled and set to go—"

Fleet? thought Grunfeld. He turned back to the board. The first and last blue telltales still glowed for

Caliban and *Starveling*. Breathe a prayer, he thought for *Moth* and *Snug*.

Something else shone on the board, something Grunfeld knew had to wrong. Three little words: SHIP ON MANUAL.

The black rim of Uranus ahead suddenly brightened along its length, which was very slightly bowed, like a section of a giant new moon. A bead formed toward the center, brightened, and then all at once the jail-yard sun had risen and was glaring coldly through its pinhole into their eyes.

They looked away from it. Grunfeld turned around.

The austere light showed the captain still in his pressure suit, only the head fallen out forward, hiding the skull features. Studying the monitor box of the captain's suit, Grunfeld saw it was set to inject the captain with power stimulants as soon as the Gravs began to slacken from their max.

He realized who had done the impossible job of piloting them out of Uranus.

But the button on the monitor, that should have glowed blue, was as dark as those of *Moth* and *Snug*.

Grunfeld thought, now he can rest.

THE SHIPS SAIL AT MIDNIGHT

This is the story of a beautiful woman.

And of a monster.

It is also the story of four silly, selfish, culture-bound inhabitants of the planet Earth. Es, who was something of an artist. Gene, who studied atoms—and fought the world and himself. Louis, who philosophized. And Larry—that's my name—who tried to write books.

It was an eerie, stifling August when we met Helen. The date is fixed in my mind because our little city had just had its mid-western sluggishness ruffled by a series of those scares that either give rise to odd-ty items in the newspapers, or else are caused by them—it's sometimes hard to tell which. People had been flying disks and heard noises in the sky—some-one from the college geology department tried un-successfully to track down a meteorite. A farmer this side of the old coal pits got all excited about some-thing "big and shapeless" that disturbed his poultry and frightened his wife, and for a couple of days men tracked around fruitlessly with shotguns—just another of those "rural monster" scares.

Even the townfolk hadn't been left out. For their imaginative enrichment they had a "Hypnotism Bur-lar," an apparently mild enough chap who blinked soft lights in people's faces and droned some siren-song outside their houses at night. For a week high-school girls squealed twice as loud after dark, men squared their shoulders adventurously at strangers, and women peered uneasily out of their bedroom windows after turning out the lights.

Louis and Es and I had picked up Gene at the college library and wanted a bite to eat before we turned in. Although by now they had almost petered out, we were talking about our local scares—a chilly hint of the supernatural makes good conversational fare in a month too hot for any real thinking. We slouched into the one decent open-all-night restaurant our dismal burg possesses (it wouldn't have that if it weren't for the "wild" college folk) and found that Benny had a new waitress.

She was really very beautiful, much too exotically beautiful for Benny's. Masses of pale gold ringlets piled high on her head. An aristocratic bone structure (from Es's greedy look I could tell she was instantly thinking sculpture). And a pair of the dreamiest, calmest eyes in the world.

She came over to our table and silently waited for our orders. Probably because her beauty flustered us we put on an elaborate version of our act of "intellectuals precisely and patiently explaining their desires to a pig-headed member of the proletariat." She listened, nodded, and presently returned with our orders.

Louis had asked for just a cup of black coffee.

She brought him a half cantaloup also.

He sat looking at it for a moment. Then he chuckled incredulously. "You know, I actually wanted that," he said. "But I didn't know I wanted it. You must have read my subconscious mind."

"What's that?" she asked in a low, lovely voice with intonations rather like Benny's.

122

Digging into his cantaloup, Louis sketched an explanation suitable for fifth-graders.

She disregarded the explanation. "What do you use it for?" she asked.

Louis, who is something of a wit, said, "I don't use it. It uses me."

"That the way it should be?" she commented.

None of us knew the answer to that one, so since I was the Gang's specialist in dealing with the lower orders, I remarked brilliantly, "What's your name?"

"Helen," she told me.

"How long have you been here?"

"Couple days," she said, starting back toward the counter.

"Where did you come from?"

She spread her hand. "Oh—places."

Whereupon Gene, whose humor inclines toward the fanatstic, asked, "Did you arrive on a flying disk?"

She glanced back at him and said, "Wise guy."

But all the same she hung around our table, filling sugar basins and what not. We made our conversation especially erudite, each of us merrily spinning his favorite web of half-understood intellectual jargon and half-baked private opinion. We were concious of her presence, all right.

Just as we were leaving, the thing happened. At the doorway something made us all look back. Helen was behind the counter. She was looking at us. Her eyes weren't dreamy at all, but focused, intent, radiant. She was smiling.

My elbow was touching Es's naked arm—we were

123

rather crowded in the doorway—and I felt her shiver. Then she gave a tiny jerk and I sensed that Gene, who was holding her other arm (they were more or less sweethearts), had tightened his grip on it.

For perhaps three seconds it stayed just like that, the four of us looking at the one of her. Then Helen shyly dropped her gaze and began to mop the counter with a rag.

We were all very quiet going home.

Next night we went back to Benny's again, rather earlier. Helen was still there, and quite as beautiful as we remembered her. We exchanged with her a few more of those brief, teasing remarks—her voice no longer sounded so much like Benny's—and staged some more intellectual pyrotechnics for her benefit. Just before we left, Es went up to her at the counter and talked to her privately for perhaps a minute, at the end of which Helen nodded.

"Ask her to pose for you?" I asked Es when we got outside.

She nodded. "That girl has the most magnificent figure in the world," she proclaimed fervently.

"Or out of it," Gene confirmed grudgingly.

"And an incredibly exciting skull," Es finished.

It was characteristic of us that Es should have been the one to really break the ice with Helen. Like most intellectuals, we were rather timid, always setting up barriers against other people. We clung to adolescence and the college, although all of us but Gene had been graduated from it. Instead of getting out into the real world, we lived by sponging off our parents and doing academic odd jobs for the professors (Es had a few private students). Here in our home city we had status, you see. We were looked upon as being frightfully clever and sophisticated, the local "bohemian set" (though Lord knows we were anything but that). Whereas out in the real world we'd have been greenhorns.

We were scared of the world, you see. Scared that it would find out that all our vaunted abilities and projects didn't amount to much—and that as for solid achievements, there just hadn't been any. Es was only a mediocre artist; she was afraid to learn from the great, especially the living great, for fear her own affected little individuality would be engulfed. Louis was no philosopher; he merely cultivated a series of intellectual enthusiasms, living in a state of feverish private—and fruitless—excitement over the thoughts of other men. My own defense against reality consisted of knowingness and a cynical attitude; I had a remarkable packrat accumulation of information; I had a line on everything—and also always knew why it wasn't worth bothering with. As for Gene, he was the best of us and also the worst. A bit younger, he still applied himself to his studies, and showed promise in nuclear physics and math. But something, perhaps his small size and puritanical farm background, had made him moody and contrary, and given him an inclination toward physical violence that threatened some day to get him into real trouble. As it was, he'd had his license taken away for reckless driving. And several times we'd had to intervene—once unsuccessfully—to keep him from getting beaten up in bars.

We talked a great deal about our "work." Actually we spent much more time reading magazines and detective stories, lazing around, getting drunk, and conducting our intellectual palavers.

If we had one real virtue, it was our loyalty to each other, though it wouldn't take a cynic to point out that we desperately needed each other for an audience. Still, there was some genuine feeling there.

In short, like many people on a planet where mind is wakening and has barely become aware of the eon-old fetters and blindfolds oppressing it, and has had just the faintest glimpse of its tremendous possible future destiny, we were badly cowed—frightened, frustrated, self-centered, slothful, vain, pretentious.

Considering how set we were getting in those attitudes, it is all the more amazing that Helen had the tremendous effect on us that she did. For within a month of meeting her, our attitude toward the whole world had sweetened, we had become genuinely interested in people instead of being frightened of them, and we were beginning to do real creative work. An astonishing achievement for an unknown little waitress!

It wasn't that she took us in hand or set us an example, or anything like that. Quite the opposite. I don't think that Helen was responsible for a half dozen positive statements (and only one really impulsive act) during the whole time we knew her. Rather, she was like a Great Books discussion leader, who never voices an opinion of his own, but only leads other people to voice theirs—playing the part of an intellectual midwife.

Louis and Gene and I would drop over to Es's, say, and find Helen getting dressed behind the screen or taking a cup of tea after a session of posing. We'd start a discussion and for a while Helen would listen dreamily, just another shadow in the high old shadowy room. But then those startling little questions of hers would begin to come, each one opening a new vista of thought. By the time the discussion was finished—which might be at the Blue Moon bar or under the campus maples or watching the water ripple in the old coal pits—we'd have got somewhere. Instead of ending in weary shoulder-shrugging or cynical grousing at the world or getting drunk out of sheer frustration, we'd finish up with a plan— some facts to check, something to write or shape or try.

And then, people! How would we ever have got close to people without Helen? Without Helen, Old Gus would have stayed an ancient and bleary-eyed dishwasher at Benny's. But with Helen, Gus became for us what he really was—a figure of romance who had sailed the Seven Seas, who had hunted for gold on the Orinoco with twenty female Indians for porters (because the males were too lazy and proud to hire out to do anything) and who had marched at the head of his Amazon band carrying a newborn baby of one of the women in his generous arms (because the women assured him that a man-child was the only burden a man might carry without dishonor).

Even Gene was softened in his attitudes. I remember once when two handsome truckdrivers tried to pick up Helen at the Blue Moon. Instantly Gene's jaw muscles bulged and his eyes went blank and he began to wag his right shoulder—and I got ready for a scene. But Helen said a word here and there, threw in a soft laugh, and began to ask the truck-drivers her questions. In ten minutes we were all at ease and the four of us found out things we'd never dreamed about dark highways and diesels and their proud, dark-souled pilots (so like Gene in their temperaments).

But it was on us as individuals that Helen's influence showed up the biggest. Es's sculptures acquired an altogether new scope. She dropped her pet mannerisms without a tear and began to take into her work whatever was sound and good. She rapidly developed a style that was classical and yet had in it something that was wholly of the future. Es is getting recognition now and her work is still good, but there was a magic about her "Helenic Period" which she can't recapture. The magic still lives in the pieces she did at that time— particularly in a nude of Helen that has all the serenity and purpose of the best ancient Egyptian work, and something much more. As we watched that piece take form, as we watched the clay grow into Helen under Es's hands, we dimly sensed that in some indescribable way Helen was growing into Es at the same time, and Es into Helen. It was such a beautiful, subtle relationship that even Gene couldn't be jealous.

At the same time Louis gave over his fickle philosophical flirtations and found the field of inquiry for which he'd always been looking—a blend of semantics and introspective psychology designed to chart the chaotic inner world of human experience. Although his present intellectual tactics lack the brilliance they had when Helen was nudging his mind he still keeps doggedly at the project, which prom-

ises to add a whole new range of words to the vo-
cabulary of psychology and perhaps of the English
language.

Gene wasn't ripe for creative work, but from being
a merely promising student he became a brilliant
and very industrious one, rather to the surprise of
his professors. Even with the cloud that now over
hangs his life and darkens his reputation, he has
managed to find worthwhile employment on one of
the big nuclear projects.

As for myself, I really began to write. Enough said.

We sometimes used to speculate as to the secret
of Helen's effect on us, though we didn't by any
means give her all the credit in those days. We had
some sort of theory that Helen was a completely
"natural" person, a "noble savage" (from the
kitchen), a bridge to the world of proletarian reality.
Es once said that Helen couldn't have had a Freud-
ian childhood, whatever she meant by that. Louis
spoke of Helen's unthinking social courage and Gene
of the catalytic effect of beauty.

Oddly, in these discussions we never referred to
that strange, electric experience we'd all had when
we first met Helen—that tearing moment when we'd
looked back from the doorway. We were always
strangely reticent there. And none of us ever voiced
the conviction that I'm sure all of us had at times:
that our social and psychoanalytic theories weren't
worth a hoot when it came to explaining Helen, that
she possessed powers of feeling and mind (mostly
concealed) that set her utterly apart from every
other inhabitant of the planet Earth, that she was
like a being from another, far saner and lovelier
world.

That conviction isn't unusual, come to think of it. It's the one every man has about the girl he loves. Which brings me to my own secret explanation of Helen's effect on me (though not on the others).

It was simply this. I loved Helen and I knew Helen loved me. And that was quite enough.

It happened scarcely a month after we'd met. We were staging a little party at Es's. Since I was the one with the car, I was assigned to pick up Helen at Benny's when she got through. On the short drive I passed a house that held unpleasant memories for me. A girl had lived there whom I'd been crazy about and who had turned me down. (No, let's be honest, I turned her down, though I very much wanted her, because of some tragic cowardice, the memory of which always sears me like a hot iron.)

Helen must have guessed something from my expression, for she said softly, "What's the matter Larry?" and then, when I ignored the question, "Something about a girl?"

She was so sympathetic about it that I broke down and told her the whole story, sitting in the parked and lightless car in front of Es's. I let myself go and lived through the whole thing again, with all its biting shame. When I was finished I looked up from the steering wheel. The streetlight made a pale aureole around Helen's head and a paler one where the white angora sweater covered her shoulders. The upper part of her face was in darkness, but a bit of light touched her full lips and narrow, almost fennec- or fox-like chin.

"You poor kid," she said softly, and the next moment we were kissing each other, and a feeling o

130

utter relief and courage and power was budding deep inside me.

A bit later she said to me something that even at the time I realized was very wise.

"Let's keep this between you and me, Larry," she said. "Let's not mention it to the others. Let's not even hint." She paused, and then added, a trifle unhappily, "I'm afraid they wouldn't appreciate it. Sometime, I hope—but not quite yet."

I knew what she meant. That Gene and Louis and even Es were only human—that is, irrational—in their jealousies, and that the knowledge that Helen was my girl would have put a damper on the exciting but almost childlike relationship of the five of us. (As the fact of Es's and Gene's love would never have done. Es was a rather cold, awkward girl, and Louis and I seldom grudged poor, angry Gene her affection.)

So when Helen and I dashed in and found the others berating Benny for making Helen work overtime, we agreed that he was an unshaven and heartless louse, and in a little while the party was going strong and we were laughing and talking unconstrainedly. No one could possibly have guessed that a new and very lovely factor had been added to the situation.

After that evening everything was different for me. I had a girl. Helen was (why not say the trite things, they're true) my goddess, my worshipper, my slave, my ruler, my inspiration, my comfort, my refuge—oh, I could write books about what she meant to me.

I guess all my life I will be writing books about that.

I could write pages describing just one of the beautiful moments we had together. I could drown myself in the bitter ghosts of sensations. Rush of sunlight through her hair. Click of her heels on a brick sidewalk. Light of her presence brightening a mean room. Chase of unearthly expressions across her sleeping face.

Yet it was on my mind that Helen's love had the greatest effect. It unfettered my thoughts, gave them passage into a far vaster cosmos.

One minute I'd be beside Helen, our hands touching lightly in the dark, a shaft of moon light from the dusty window silvering her hair. The next, my mind would be a million miles up, hovering like an iridescent insect over the million bright worlds of existence.

Or I'd be surmounting walls inside my mind—craggy, dire ramparts that have been there since the days of the cave man.

Or the universe would become a miraculous web, with Time the spider. I couldn't see all of it—no creature could see a trillionth of it in all eternity—but I would have a sense of it all.

Sometimes the icy beauty of those moments would become too great, and I'd feel a sudden chill of terror. Then the scene around me would become a nightmare and I'd half expect Helen's eyes to show a catlike gleam and slit, or her hair to come rustlingly alive, or her arms to writhe bonelessly, or her splendid skin to slough away, revealing some black and antlike form of dread.

Then the moment would pass and everything would be sheer loveliness again, richer for the fleeting terror.

132

My mind is hobbled once more now, but I still know the taste of the inward freedom that Helen's love brought.

You might think from this that Helen and I had a lot of times alone together. We hadn't—we couldn't have, with the Gang. But we had enough. Helen was clever at arranging things. They never suspected us.

Lord knows there were times I yearned to let the Gang in on our secret. But then I would remember Helen's warning and see the truth of it.

Let's face it. We're all of us a pretty vain and possessive people. As individuals, we cry for attention. We jockey for admiration. We swim or sing according to whether we feel we're being worshipped or merely liked. We demand too much of the person we love. We want them to be a never-failing prop to our ego.

And then if we're lonely and happen to see someone else loved, the greedy child wakes, the savage stirs, the frustrated Puritan clenches his teeth. We seethe, we resent, we hate.

No, I saw that I couldn't tell the others about Helen and myself. Not Louis. Not even Es. And as for Gene, I'm afraid that with his narrow-minded upbringing, he'd have been deeply shocked by what he'd have deduced about our relationship. We were supposed, you know, to be "wild" young people, "bohemians." Actually we were quite straightlaced— Gene especially, the rest of us almost as much.

I knew how I would have felt if Helen had happened to become Louis's or Gene's girl. That says it.

To tell the truth, I felt a great deal of admiration

for the Gang, because they could do alone what I was only doing with Helen's love. They were enlarging their minds, becoming creative, working and playing hard—and doing it without my reward. Frankly, I don't know how I could have managed it myself without Helen's love. My admiration for Louis, Es, and Gene was touched with a kind of awe.

And we really were getting places. We had created a new mind-spot on the world, a sprouting-place for thought that wasn't vain or self-conscious, but concerned wholly with its work and its delights. The Gang was forming itself into a kind of lens for viewing the world, outside and in.

Any group of people can make themselves into that sort of lens, if they really want to. But somehow they seldom get started. They don't have the right inspiration.

We had Helen.

Always, but mostly in unspoken thoughts, we'd come back to the mystery of how she had managed it. She was mysterious, all right. We'd known her some six months now, and we were as much in the dark about her background as when we first met her. She wouldn't tell anything even to me. She'd come from "places." She was a "drifter." She liked "people." She told us all sorts of fascinating incidents, but whether she'd been mixed up in them herself or just heard them at Benny's (she could have made a Trappist jabber) was uncertain.

We sometimes tried to get her to talk about her past. But she dodged our questions easily and we didn't like to press them.

You don't cross-examine Beauty.

You don't demand that a Great Books discussion leader state his convictions.

You don't probe a goddess about her past.

Yet this vagueness about Helen's past caused us a certain uneasiness. She'd drifted to us. She might drift away.

If we hadn't been so involved in our thought-sprouting, we'd have been worried. And if I hadn't been so happy, and everything so smoothly perfect, I'd have done more than occasionally ask Helen to marry me and hear her answer, "Not now, Larry."

Yes, she was mysterious.

And she had her eccentricities.

For one thing, she insisted on working at Benny's although she could have had a dozen better jobs. Benny's was her window on the main street of life, she said.

For another, she'd go off on long hikes in the country, even in the snowiest weather. I met her coming back from one and was worried, tried to be angry. But she only smiled.

Yet, when spring came round again and burgeoned into summer, she would never go swimming with us in our favorite coal pit.

The coal pits are a place where they once strip-mined for the stuff where it came to the surface. Long ago the huge holes were left to fill with water and their edges to grow green with grass and trees. They're swell for swimming.

But Helen would never go to our favorite, which was one of the biggest and yet the least visited— and this year the water was unusually high. We changed to suit her, of course, but because the one she didn't like happened to be near the farmhouse of last August's "rural monster" scare, Louis joshed her.

"Maybe a monster haunts the pool," he said. "Maybe it's a being come from another world on a flying disk."

He happened to say that on a lazy afternoon when we'd been swimming at the new coal pit and were drying on the edge, having cigarettes. Louis' remark started us speculating about creatures from another world coming secretly to visit Earth—their problems, especially how they'd disguise themselves.

"Maybe they'd watch from a distance," Gene said. "Television, supersensitive microphones."

"Or clairvoyance, clairaudience," Es chimed, being rather keen on para-psychology.

"But to really mingle with people . . ." Helen murmured. She was stretched on her back in white bra and trunks, looking deep into the ranks of marching clouds. Her olive skin tanned to an odd hue that went bewitchingly with her hair. With a sudden and frightening poignancy I was aware of the catlike perfection of her slim body.

"The creature might have some sort of elaborate plastic disguise," Gene began doubtfully.

"It might have a human form to begin with," I ventured. "You know, the idea that Earth folk are decayed interstellar colonists."

"It might take possession of some person here," Louis cut in. "Insinuate its mind or even itself into the human being."

"Or it might grow itself a new body," Helen murmured sleepily.

That was one of the half dozen positive statements she ever made.

Then we got to talking about the motives of such an alien being. Whether it would try to destroy men, or look on us as cattle, or study us, or amuse itself with us, or what not.

Here Helen joined in again, distant-eyed but smiling. "I know you've all laughed at the comic-book idea of some Martian monster lusting after beautiful white women. But has it ever occurred to you that a creature from outside might simply and honestly fall in love with you?"

That was another of Helen's rare positive statements.

The idea was engaging and we tried to get Helen to expand it, but she wouldn't. In fact, she was rather silent the rest of that day.

As the summer began to mount toward its crests of heat and growth, the mystery of Helen began to possess us more often—that, and a certain anxiety about her.

There was a feeling in the air, the sort of uneasiness that cats and dogs get when they are about to lose their owner.

Without exactly knowing it, without a definite word being said, we were afraid we might lose Helen.

Partly it was Helen's own behavior. For once she showed a kind of restlessness, or rather preoccupation. At Benny's she no longer took such an interest in "people."

She seemed to be trying to solve some difficult personal problem, nerve herself to make some big decision.

Once she looked at us and said, "You know, I lik

you kids terribly." Said it the way a person says it when he knows he may have to lose what he likes.

And then there was the business of the Stranger.

Helen had been talking quite a bit with a strange man, not at Benny's, but walking in the streets, which was unusual. We didn't know who the Stranger was. We hadn't actually seen him face to face. Just heard about him from Benny and glimpsed him once or twice. Yet he worried us.

Understand, our happiness went on, yet faintly veiling it was this new and ominous mist.

Then one night the mist took definite shape. It happened on an occasion of celebration. After a few days during which we'd sensed they'd been quarreling, Es and Gene suddenly announced that they were getting married. On an immediate impulse we'd all gone to the Blue Moon.

We were having the third round of drinks, and kidding Es because she didn't seem very enthusiastic, almost a bit grumpy—when he came in.

Even before he looked our way, before he drifted up to our table, we knew that this was the Stranger.

He was a rather slender man, fair haired like Helen. Otherwise he didn't look like her, yet there was a sense of kinship. Perhaps it lay in his poise, his wholly casual manner.

As he came up, I could feel myself and the others getting tense, like dogs at the approach of the unknown.

The Stranger stopped by our table and stood looking at Helen as if he knew her. The four of us realized more than ever that we wanted Helen to be ours alone (and especially mine), that we hated to think of her having close ties with anyone else.

What got especially under my skin was the suggestion that there was some kinship between the Stranger and Helen, that behind his proud, remote-eyed face, he was talking to her with his mind.

Gene apparently took the Stranger for one of those unpleasant fellows who strut around bars looking for trouble—and proceeded to act as if he were one of those same fellows himself. He screwed his delicate features into a cheap frown and stood up as tall as he could, which wasn't much. Such tough-guy behavior, always a symptom of frustration and doubts of masculinity, had been foreign to Gene for some months. I felt a pulse of sadness—and almost winced when Gene opened the side of his mouth and began, "Now look here, Joe—"

But Helen laid her hand on his arm. She looked calmly at the Stranger for a few more moments and then she said, "I won't talk to you that way. You must speak English."

If the Stranger was surprised, he didn't show it. He smiled and said softly, with a faint foreign accent, "The ship sails at midnight, Helen."

I got a queer feeling, for our city is two hundred miles from anything you'd call navigable waters.

For a moment I felt what you might call supernatural fear. The bar so tawdry and dim, the line of hunched neurotic shoulders, the plump dice-girl at one end and the tiny writhing television screen at the other. And against that background, Helen and the Stranger, light-haired, olive-skinned, with proud feline features, facing each other like duelists, on guard, opposed, yet sharing some secret knowledge. Like two aristocrats come to a dive to settle a quarrel—like that, and something more, As I say, it frightened me.

"Are you coming, Helen?" the Stranger asked.

And now I was really frightened. It was as if I'd realized for the first time just how terribly much Helen meant to all of us, and to me especially. Not just the loss of her, but the loss of things in me that only she could call into being. I could see the same fear in the faces of the others. A lost look in Gene's eyes behind the fake gangster frown. Louis' fingers relaxing from his glass and his chunky head turning toward the stranger, slowly, with empty gaze, like the turret-guns of a battleship. Es starting to stub out her cigarette and then hesitating, her eyes on Helen—although in Es's case I felt there was another emotion besides fear.

"Coming?" Helen echoed, like someone in a dream.

The Stranger waited. Helen's reply had twisted the tension tighter. Now Es did stub her cigarette with awkward haste, then quickly drew back her hand. I felt suddenly that this had been bound to happen, that Helen must have had her life, her real life, before we had known her, and that the Stranger was part of it; that she had come to us mysteriously and now would leave us mysteriously. Yes, I felt all of that, although in view of what had happened between Helen and me, I knew I shouldn't have.

"Have you considered everything?" the Stranger asked finally.

"Yes," Helen replied.

"You know that after tonight there'll be no going back," he continued as softly as ever. "You know that you'll be marooned here forever, that you'll have to spend the rest of your life among . . ." (he looked around at us as if searching for a word) ". . . among barbarians."

Again Helen laid her hand on Gene's arm, although her glance never left the Stranger's face.

"What is the attraction, Helen?" the Stranger went on. "Have you really tried to analyze it? I know it might be fun for a month, or a year, or even five years. A kind of game, a renewal of youth. But when it's over and you're tired of the game, when you realize that you're alone, completely alone, and that there's no going back ever—Have you thought of that?"

"Yes, I have thought of all that," Helen said, as quietly as the Stranger, but with a tremendous finality. "I won't try to explain it to you, because with all your wisdom and cleverness I don't think you'd quite understand. And I know I'm breaking promises. But I'm not going back. I'm here with my friends, my true and equal friends, and I'm not going back."

And then it came, and I could tell it came to all of us—a great big lift, like a surge of silent music or a glow of invisible light. Helen had at last declared herself. After the faint equivocations and reservations of the spring and summer, she had put herself squarely on our side. We each of us knew that what she had said she meant wholly and forever. She was ours, ours more completely than ever before. Our quasi-goddess, our inspiration, our key to a widening future; the one who always understood, who could open doors in our imaginations and feelings that would otherwise have remained forever shut. She was our Helen now, ours and (as my mind persisted in adding exultingly) especially mine.

And we? We were the Gang again, happy, poised, wise as Heaven and clever as Hell, out to celebrate, having fun with whatever came along.

The whole scene had changed. The frightening aura around the Stranger had vanished completely. He was just another of those hundreds of odd people whom we met when we were with Helen.

He acted almost as if he were conscious of it. He smiled and said quickly. "Very well. I had a feeling you'd decide this way." He started to move off. Then, "Oh, by the way, Helen—"

"Yes?"

"The others wanted me to say goodby to you for them."

"Tell them the same and the best of luck."

The Stranger nodded and again started to turn away, when Helen added, "And you?"

The Stranger looked back.

"I'll be seeing you once more before midnight," he said lightly, and almost the next moment, it seemed, was out the door.

We all chuckled. I don't know why. Partly from relief, I suppose, and partly—God help us!—in triumph over the Stranger. One thing I'm sure of: three (and maybe even four) of us felt for a moment happier and more secure in our relationship to Helen than we ever had before. It was the peak. We were together. The Stranger had been vanquished, and all the queer unspoken threats he had brought with him. Helen had declared herself. The future stood open before us, full of creation and achievement, with Helen ready to lead us into it. For a moment everything was perfect. We were mankind, vibrantly alive, triumphantly progressing.

It was, as I say, perfect.

And only human beings know how to wreck perfection.

Only human beings are so vain, so greedy, each wanting everything for himself alone.

It was Gene who did it. Gene who couldn't stand so much happiness and who had to destroy it, from what self-fear, what Puritanical self-torment, what death-wish I don't know.

It was Gene, but it might have been any of us.

His face was flushed. He was smiling, grinning rather, in what I now realize was an oafish and overbearing complacency. He put his hand on Helen's arm in a way none of us had ever touched Helen before, and said, "That was great, dear."

It wasn't so much what he said as the naked possessiveness of the gesture. It was surely that gesture of ownership that made Es explode, that started her talking in a voice terribly bitter, but so low it was some moments before the rest of us realized what she was getting at.

When we did we were thunderstruck.

She was accusing Helen of having stolen Gene's love.

It's hard to make anyone understand the shock we felt. As if someone had accused a goddess of abominations.

Es lit another cigarette with shaking fingers, and finished up.

"I don't want your pity, Helen. I don't want Gene

married off to me for the sake of appearances, like some half-discarded mistress. I like you, Helen, but not enough to let you take Gene away from me and then toss him back—or half toss him back. No, I draw the line at that."

And she stopped as if her emotions had choked her.

As I said, the rest of us were thunderstruck. But not Gene. His face got redder still. He slugged down the rest of his drink and looked around at us, obviously getting ready to explode in turn.

Helen had listened to Es with a half smile and an unhappy half frown, shaking her head from time to time. Now she shot Gene a warning, imploring glance, but he disregarded it.

"No, Helen," he said, "Es is right. I'm glad she spoke. It was a mistake for us to hide our feelings. It would have been a ten times worse mistake if I'd kept that crazy promise I made you to marry Es. You go too much by pity, Helen, and pity's no use in managing an affair like this. I don't want to hurt Es, but she'd better know right now that it's another marriage we're announcing tonight."

I sat there speechless. I just couldn't realize that that drunken, red-faced poppinjay was claiming that Helen was his girl, his wife to be.

Es didn't look at him. "You cheap little beast," she whispered.

Gene went white at that, but he kept on smiling.

"Es may not forgive me for this," he said harshly, "but I don't think it's me she's jealous of. What gets under her skin is not so much losing me to Helen as losing Helen to me."

Then I could find words.

But Louis was ahead of me.

He put his hand firmly on Gene's shoulder.

"You're drunk, Gene," he said, "and you're talking like a drunken fool. Helen's my girl."

They started up, both of them, Louis's hand still on Gene's shoulder.

Then, instead of hitting each other, they looked at me.

Because I had risen too.

"But . . ." I began, and faltered.

Without my saying it, they knew.

Louis's hand dropped away from Gene.

All of us looked at Helen. A cold, terribly hurt, horribly disgusted look.

Helen blushed and looked down. Only much later did I realize it was related to the look she'd given the four of us that first night at Benny's.

". . . but I fell in love with all of you," she said softly.

Then we did speak, or rather Gene spoke for us. I hate to admit it, but at the time I felt a hot throb of pleasure at all the unforgivable things he called Helen. I wanted to see the lash laid on, the stones thud.

Finally he called her some names that were a little worse.

Then Helen did the only impulsive thing I ever knew her to do.

She slapped Gene's face. Once. Hard.

There are only two courses a person can take when he's been rebuked by a goddess, even a fallen goddess. He can grovel and beg forgiveness. Or he can turn apostate and devil-worshipper.

145

Gene did the latter.

He walked out of the Blue Moon, blundering like a blind drunk.

That broke up the party, and Gus and the other bartender, who'd been about to interfere, returned relievedly to their jobs.

Louis went off to the bar. Es followed him. I went to the far end myself, under the writhing television screen, and ordered a double scotch.

Beyond the dozen intervening pairs of shoulders, I could see that Es was trying to act shameless. She was whispering things to Louis. At the same time, and even more awkwardly, she was flirting with one of the other men. Every once in a while she would laugh shrilly, mirthlessly.

Helen didn't move. She just sat at the table, looking down, the half smile fixed on her lips. Once Gus approached her, but she shook her head.

I ordered another double scotch. Suddenly my mind began to work furiously on three levels.

On the first I was loathing Helen. I was seeing that all she'd done for us, all the mind-spot, all the house of creativity we'd raised together, had been based on a lie. Helen was unutterably cheap, common.

Mostly, on that level, I was grieving for the terrible wrong I felt she'd done me.

The second level was entirely different. There an icy spider had entered my mind from realms undreamt. There sheer supernatural terror reigned. For there I was adding up all the little hints of strangeness we'd had about Helen. The Stranger's words had touched it off and now a thousand details began to drop into place: the coincidence of her arrival

146

with the flying disk, rural monster, and hypnotism scare; her interest in people, like that of a student from a far land; the impression she gave of possessing concealed powers; her pains never to say anything definite, as if she were on guard against imparting some forbidden knowledge; her long hikes into the country; her aversion for the big and yet seldom-visited coal pit (big and deep enough to float a liner or hide a submarine); above all, that impression of unearthliness she'd at times given us all, even when we were most under her spell.

And now this matter of a ship sailing at midnight. From the Great Plains.

What sort of ship?

On that level my mind shrank from facing the obvious result of its labor. It was too frighteningly incredible, too far from the world of the Blue Moon and Benny's and cheap little waitresses.

The third level was far mistier, but it was there. At least I tell myself it was there. On this third level I was beginning to see Helen in a better light and the rest of us in a worse. I was beginning to see the lovelessness behind our idea of love—and the faithfulness, to the best in us, behind Helen's faithlessness. I was beginning to see how hateful, how like spoiled children, we'd been acting.

Of course, maybe there wasn't any third level in my mind at all. Maybe that only came afterwards. Maybe I'm just trying to flatter myself that I was a little more discerning, a little "bigger" than the others.

Yet I like to think that I turned away from the bar and took a couple of steps toward Helen, that it was only those "second level" fears that slowed me so that I'd only taken those two faltering steps (if I took them) before—

Before Gene walked in.

I remember the clock said eleven thirty.

Gene's face was dead white, and knobby with tension.

His hand was in his pocket.

He never looked at anyone but Helen. They might have been alone. He wavered—or trembled. Then a terrible spasm of energy stiffened him. He started toward the table.

Helen got up and walked toward him, her arms outstretched. In her half smile were all the compassion and fatalism—and love—I can imagine there being in the universe.

Gene pulled a gun out of his pocket and shot Helen six times. Four times in the body, twice in the head.

She hung for a moment, then pitched forward into the blue smoke. It puffed away from her to either side and we saw her lying on her face, one of her outstretched hands touching Gene's shoe.

Then, before a woman could scream, before Gus and the other chap could jump the bar, the outside door of the Blue Moon opened and the Stranger came in. After that none of us could have moved or spoken. We cringed from his eyes like guilty dogs.

It wasn't that he looked anger at us, or hate, or even contempt. That would have been much easier to bear.

No, even as the Stranger passed Gene—Gene, pistol dangling from two fingers, looking down in dumb horror, edging his toe back by terrified inches from Helen's dead hand—even as the Stranger sent Gene a glance, it was the glance a man might give a bull that has gored a child, a pet ape that has torn up his mistress in some inscrutable and pettish animal rage.

And as, without a word, the Stranger picked Helen up in his arms, and carried her silently through the thinning blue smoke into the street, his face bore that same look of tragic regret, of serene acceptance.

That's almost all there is to my story. Gene was arrested, of course, but it's not easy to convict a man of murder of a woman without real identity.

For Helen's body was never found. Neither was the Stranger.

Eventually Gene was released and, as I've said, is making a life for himself, despite the cloud over his reputation.

We see him now and then, and try to console him, tell him it might as easily have been Es or Louis or I, that we were all blind, selfish fools together.

And we've each of us got back to our work. The sculptures, the word-studies, the novels, the nuclear notions are not nearly as brilliant as when Helen was with us. But we keep turning them out. We tell ourselves Helen would like that.

And our minds all work now at the third level— but only by fits and starts, fighting the jungle blindness and selfishness that are closing in again. Still, at our best, we understand Helen and what Helen was trying to do, what she was trying to bring the world even if the world wasn't ready for it. We glimpse that strange passion that made her sacrifice all the stars for four miserable blind-worms.

But mostly we grieve for Helen, together and

alone. We know there won't be another Helen for a hundred thousand years, if then. We know that she's gone a lot farther than the dozens or thousands of light-years her body's been taken for burial. We look at Es's statue of Helen, we read one or two of my poems to her. We remember, our minds come half alive and are tortured by the thought of what they might have become if we'd kept Helen. We picture her again sitting in the shadows of Es's studio, or sunning herself on the grassy banks after a swim, or smiling at us at Benny's. And we grieve.

For we know you get only one chance at someone like Helen.

We know that because, half an hour after the Stranger carried Helen's body from the Blue Moon, a great meteor went flaming and roaring across the countryside (some say up from the countryside and out toward the stars) and the next day it was discovered that the waters of the coal pit Helen wouldn't swim in, had been splashed as if by the downward blow of a giant's fist, across the fields for a thousand yards.

FRITZ LEIBER